John Locke is a *New York Times* bestselling author, and was the first self-published author in history to hit the number 1 spot on Kindle. He is the author of the Donovan Creed and Emmett Love series. He lives in Kentucky.

***** Worthy of 6 Stars! By TRW
I give 5 stars to all John Locke books, I would give 6 stars to this one if I could. Not only is it a page turning thriller – I read the whole thing on the beach in an afternoon – couldn't put it down.

***** A fun read! By Kathy
This novel is chock-full of surprising plot twists and turns from beginning to end. It grips you from page one. I read this book in one evening. It's a fast, fun read for sure.

***** Bingo! Cool. Read this book and you're hooked on Locke. By Karin
Locke keeps the story moving and in such an effortless way. I'm passing it on to my husband. It's been awhile since I've read something sexy: this fits the bill.

***** So Entertaining I just went and downloaded another one. By Patti Roberts
I read this book over a period of 2 days on my Kindle and loved it! So I have just downloaded another one. I hereby declare that I am a John Locke fan. Do yourself a favor…

***** Life equals Experimentation. By Jean I just couldn't put the book down. Must Read!

***** 10 stars. By Ally
A wonderful mystery thriller. I love all of them but I think this is just my favorite.

AMAZON.COM

***** I loved this book. By D Loewe
I don't write reviews, I just don't. But after reading this book I enjoyed it so much I felt the author deserved a positive review. I will not go into the plot or such, but I could not put this thing down. Well done Mr. Locke and thank you.

***** OMG!! By Kimberly Morris
What a ride...wow. The first jaw falling open moment in a book that I recall ever having experienced.

*****5 out of 5 stars. By Mr C. Headle
I thought Lethal People was amazing so I read Lethal Experiment and officially became addicted to the series. A marvel combination of action, drama, and breath-taking excitement. I love how Donovan Creed constantly keeps us wanting more. Do yourself a favor and grab this book!

***** Don't even bother trying to catch your breath! By Karin Gambaro
From the moment I started reading this book, I was hooked on Donovan Creed! This was my first Donovan Creed experience, and I can't wait to dive into the rest of the series. This guy is the hero I've been waiting for! Thanks, John Locke!

*****Incredible! By Amethyst
Man oh man alive. Donovan Creed is an absolutely perfect character.

THE DONOVAN CREED SERIES

LETHAL PEOPLE
LETHAL EXPERIMENT
SAVING RACHEL
NOW & THEN
WISH LIST
A GIRL LIKE YOU
VEGAS MOON
THE LOVE YOU CRAVE
MAYBE
CALLIE'S LAST DANCE

WISH LIST

JOHN LOCKE

This edition first published in the UK in 2013 by Head of Zeus Ltd

9 7 5 3 1 2 4 6 8

A CIP catalogue record for this book is available from the British Library.

ISBN (Paperback): 9781781852385
ISBN (eBook): 9781781852392

Printed and bound by CPI Group (UK) Ltd, Croydon, CR0 4YY

Head of Zeus Ltd
Clerkenwell House
45-47 Clerkenwell Green
London EC1R 0HT

www.headofzeus.com

To us, and those just like us.
Damn few of us. Pity, that.

ACKNOWLEDGMENTS

I would like to thank those who provided guidance, support, suggestions, and critical reading skills for this project, including Winslow Eliot, Claudia Jackson, Ricky Locke, Courtney Baxter, Claude Bouchard, Joanne Chase, Jessica Brown, Libby Crew, Terri Himes, and Donovan Creed.

PROLOGUE

Donovan Creed

WE'D MET ON the Internet, exchanged emails, and she was married. But she accepted a dinner date anyway, and showed up. We toasted, talked, flirted unmercifully, shared a sissy dessert, and then went to my room for a nightcap. The drinks came and went, then we cuddled and kissed and I started to undo her blouse and she said, "I can't."

"Can't what?"

"Do this."

"Why not?"

She looked as though she didn't mean it, but said, "It's not right."

"Oh."

"Don't be mad."

"I'm not. I thought things were going well. I was wrong."

"It's not that. Really, it's just, we shouldn't do this."

"It's me?"

"No, of course not! You're incredible! I've had a wonderful time."

"But things could have gone better tonight. For you, I mean."

"No, that's not it. Look, I promise, it's not you."

I nodded. "Can I ask you something?"

"Yes, of course."

"Did you buy a new bra and panties before coming here?"

"What?"

"I'm just curious. You don't have to show me or anything, I was just wondering if your underwear is new."

She blushed. "It is. It's new."

"And you bought it when?"

"What difference does it make?"

I said nothing.

She said, "Two days ago. What's your point?"

"So…two days ago you thought it might be okay for you to take your clothes off if things went well between us, but now it's not okay. And the only thing that's different is we've met and spent some time together, which you say was incredible."

She started to say something but changed her mind, then closed her eyes tightly and winced, as if trying to compute something mathematically.

"Oh, hell," she said, "Let's just do it and get it over with!"

"Let's," I said.

I started working the buttons on her blouse with renewed vigor, giving her little time to regret her decision. I got the damn thing off, along with her bra, meaning, I'd just gotten to the good part when my cell phone vibrated on the nightstand.

"You need to get that?" she said.

I grabbed my knife from under the pillow and plunged it through the center of the phone in a motion so quick it should have impressed the shit out of her. In retrospect I guess she hadn't expected the knife or my ability to use it.

She ran to the door screaming, clutching her bra and blouse to her chest. She was fidgety, and it took a while to get the door unlocked, but when she realized I wasn't chas-ing her she paused to put her clothes on, while keeping a wary eye on me.

I was aware of all this, but I was more interested in my cell phone.

It was still ringing.

I pried the knife loose and answered it.

"Creed."

"Mr. Creed, this is Buddy Pancake. I'm in trouble."

To the girl in my room I said, "Wait. You lost an earring." It was a large gold hoop, probably bought at the same time she bought the underwear. I slid it on the blade of my knife and hurled it in her direction. She shrieked as it stuck in the door frame and vibrated back and forth. It was a good throw, one that should have dazzled her, landing as it had a mere two inches from her face.

"Buddy," I said, "You're a pain in the ass."

"Sorry, Mr. Creed."

My date angrily tried to pry the knife out of the door frame, but I'd thrown it too hard. She gave up, opened the door, and, rather rudely I thought, flipped her middle finger at me before leaving.

I said, "What kind of trouble have you gotten yourself into this time, Buddy?"

"The worst kind."

I sighed. "Where are you?"

PART ONE

BUDDY PANCAKE

INTRODUCTION

ON APRIL 8, 2010, custom motorcycle builder Jesse James was voted "The Most Hated Man in America," for cheating on America's Sweetheart, actress Sandra Bullock.

The story broke three days after Sandra won the Oscar for Best Actress for her performance in *The Blind Side*.

The Academy Awards had been held Sunday, March 7, at Hollywood's Kodak Theatre. In attendance that night were a number of famous beauties, including Mariska Hargitay, Kate Winslet, Maria Menounos, Demi Moore, Jinny Kidwell, Amanda Seyfried, and Charlize Theron.

If you're lucky enough to be a world famous actress, *and* one of the world's most beautiful women, you might not say it out loud, but secretly you know you can have any man on the planet.

For this reason, the entire world would be stunned to know that five days after Sandra Bullock won her Oscar, a balding, pudgy, middle class nobody named Buddy Pancake managed to do something only three men in the entire world had done.

He fucked Jinny Kidwell.

How did a man like this wind up in bed with Jinny Kidwell?

Simple.

He wished it.

1.

THIS WHOLE THING started the way things often do: a few guys hanging out together on a Sunday afternoon, talking about pussy.

It's early March, and we're three underachievers, soft, wimpy, mid-management worker bees, sitting in the basement of my split-level ranch, in the room I like to call my office. There's an old college couch in here, and a black, faux-leather bean bag chair. An ancient, but working, TV sits atop a maple desk I salvaged from my neighbor's yard sale last summer. It's not fancy, but it's mine, and has a matching chair. The room's only window shows half dirt, half sky. It's split horizontally, and the top half pushes open about six inches, just enough to let the weed smoke out.

By way of introduction, I'm Buddy Pancake.

I'll pause a minute, while you bust my balls. Go ahead, ask me if Pancake is my real name.

It is.

Ask me "What's Mrs. Butterworth?"

I don't know. What, maybe five bucks?

Hilarious.

Move along to where I live.

Yeah, that's right. The Pancake House.

I know. You got a million more.

Do me a favor. Put the pancake thing on hold while I tell

my story. You won't be sorry, it's a helluva story.

For five days I was the luckiest man in the world.

And then I wasn't.

2.

LIKE I SAID, here we are, me, Mike and Richie, in my basement office. My wife, Lissie, on her way home with a pound of pasta and a bottle of Patsy's All Natural Puttanesca Sauce.

Me, telling my friends the origin of the name puttanesca: "It means Whore's Sauce."

"Oh, bullshit," Mike says.

I pass him the joint and say, "No, for real. Puttanesca was a cheap, quick dish Italian hookers made between tricks. The ingredients can be found in any Italian larder."

"Listen to you," Richie says. "Larder. Jeez. How gay is that?"

I flip my middle finger in response.

Mike, pensive, says, "Ever been with one?"

"What, a hooker?"

"Yeah."

"Get real," I say.

Mike passes the torch to Richie, and we're quiet a minute, thinking about doing it with a hooker.

Mike breaks the silence. "Well, you got Lissie. Don't know how you managed it, but who needs a hooker when you got a looker, eh?"

We laugh, take another hit off our communal joint, blow it in the general direction of the window, and chase it with a swallow of scotch.

"But say you didn't have Lissie," Mike persists. "Who would you want?"

"Whaddya mean?"

Richie, getting into it: "Say you can have any chick in the world. Who would you choose?"

"Wait," I say, "You mean like for one night? Who would I want to fuck?"

My friends nod.

"Hell, I don't know."

"You don't *know*?" Mike says.

"I mean, I never thought about it."

"Oh, bullshit!" Richie says. "I know who *I'd* take."

Richie knows we're looking at him, so he makes us wait a few seconds. Then he says, "Megan Fox."

Mike nods. "Yeah, okay. I thought you were gonna say Angelina Jolie, but yeah, Megan's hot. Me? I'd take Katrina Bowden."

"Who?"

"Chick on *30 Rock*."

"Oh, right. Wait. The receptionist?"

"Yeah."

"Yeah, she's hot. Great ass."

Richie locks onto my eyes, says, "Your turn."

I smile. I'm with friends, and know that the words I'm about to utter will never be heard by my wife. I take a deep breath and say, "Jinny Kidwell."

"Whoa," Richie says. "Oh, shit. Yeah, okay, you win."

We sit there grinning like monkeys flinging shit through a cage, thinking about pounding Jinny Kidwell.

Yeah, *that* Jinny Kidwell, the twenty-five million per movie one.

"What else would you wish for?" Mike says.

"I get Jinny Kidwell for one night?" Richie says, "I don't need nothin' else. Game over. I die a happy man."

"Yeah," Mike says, "but in addition to sleeping with Jinny Kidwell, say you can have anything in the world."

I realize Mike is talking to me.

"What," I say, "You mean like a genie grants me three wishes?"

"Yeah, like that. Only let's say it's four wishes. What would you ask for?"

"Easy. A million bucks."

Mike takes a hit, holds it, then exhales loudly. "Okay, sure. But then what?"

"What, a million bucks and sex with Jinny Kidwell ain't enough for you?"

"Not if I got two more wishes coming. What else would you wish for?"

"Wait," I say. "Where's this bullshit coming from?"

Richie and Mike look at each other.

Mike says, "We found this website called Wish List. It's like a survey. You type in your wishes and they compile them and tell you the most popular ones. It's updated every day."

"This is guys only, right?" I say. "'Cause chicks are gonna put down stupid shit."

I don't normally talk this way in real life. Mike and Richie probably don't either. But when we're together we talk the way we used to, growing up in the South End. It's comfortable. We're hard working guys, stuck in deadend jobs. We're a hell of a lot smarter than we sound on afternoons like this when we're passing a joint around, shooting the shit.

"There's a guy list and a chick list," Richie says.

"You guys fill it out?"

"Naw," Richie says. "But it's fun to think about."

Mike says, "I did."

We look at him like, *no shit?*

"Yeah, I filled it out. It's just a flippin' survey, right?" He shrugs his shoulders. "What's the big deal?"

Lissie's home now. From the kitchen, we hear her shout, "Buddy? Want to help me with dinner?"

Richie grabs his crotch and says, "*I'd* like to help her with dinner!"

Mike says, "Jesus, Richie, show some respect. She's Buddy's *wife!*"

I glance at Mike, thinking there's something weird in the way he said it, like he was really pissed. Hey, if anyone should have been angry…

"Hey, sorry man," Richie says. "It's the weed. You know I'm just acting out."

"Bygones," I say.

Mike stares at me a long moment, then stubs out the joint, puts the butt in his pocket, and stands up. Gives me a bro hug and says, "Check it out: Wish List.bz. Let me know what you wish for."

3.

MY FRIENDS LEAVE. I'm in the kitchen, checking out Lissie's ass while salting the water for the pasta.

I'm thinking Mike's right about Lissie being top of the food chain in my pond. I take a minute to wonder how a beautiful, kind, loving woman like her winds up with a fat fuck like me. Well, I'm not *fat* fat, but compared to the guys Lissie could get, I may as well be the *Hindenburg*.

Anyway, here's the thing about me: I'm ungrateful as hell. Here I am, an average guy with a cartoon last name and a shit job I'm on the verge of losing. I hit the lottery when Lissie fell for me—and it's still not enough.

I know I've already achieved the pinnacle with Lissie, but I'm thinking about Jinny Kidwell anyway. I try not to, but there she is, fixed in my brain, like a pregnant woman craving Twinkies at two a.m.

I know it's nuts. I mean, come on—Jinny *Kidwell*?

Of *course* it's nuts. But I've studied enough biology to know that a half million years of evolution has hard-wired my brain with the biological imperative to spread my seed with the highest genetic code available, and...

Christ, listen to me. I embarrass myself sometimes.

Forget my biological imperative. It's not utter bullshit, but I don't know enough about it to make a winning case to a female jury. Nevertheless, there is something utterly compelling about Jinny Kidwell. You know it, I know it, and Hollywood knows it. Or they wouldn't pay her twenty-five mil to star in movies, and we wouldn't pay ten times that to see her in them.

I know there is no way in the world I will ever have sex with Jinny Kidwell. If she and I are stuck in an elevator and the world is coming to an end it won't happen. If we emerge from that same elevator to find we're the last two people on earth—it's still a no. I know with every fiber of my being there is no set of circumstances on earth that could result in the two of us being in bed, in a sexual situation, with her consent.

And yet...

And yet it *did* happen, five days later.

But wait. I'm getting ahead of myself.

Dinner's over and I'm in the kitchen, watching Lissie bend at the waist to pick a bit of lettuce off the floor. I'm staring at her long, tanned legs looking for a flash of panty. Her dress doesn't hike that high, but I see it in my mind anyway. Now she's tossing the lettuce into the sink, asking me if the puttanesca had been hot enough.

I nod. It's all hot in the kitchen this night, and in my mind my wife's legs are Jinny Kidwell's, and I'm allowing myself to keep the image there because it's fun and it's certainly not the same as cheating. There's no way I'm ever going to be in the same room with Jinny, much less in the same bed, so it's not cheating, right?

I'm only thinking all this about Jinny because there's something about the idea of putting her name on a wish list that makes it seem almost possible, and that's what it's all about. I mean, when you're a guy, and you're alone and thinking about sex, you can either look at porn or create a fantasy in your mind. But the fantasy has to be based on something plausible in order to work. What I'm saying is, if

I'm alone and seeking relief, my mind can only create a plausible connection with Jinny Kidwell if there's some type of outside influence. But thinking about the wish list, and having verbalized it with Richie and Mike, I've caused Jinny to move into the realm of visualization.

And if you can visualize it…

Lissie likes watching the Academy Awards. I usually let her do it alone, but I remember from the promo that Jinny Kidwell is one of the presenters tonight. When the time comes for Jinny's entrance, the cameras are all over her. She's wearing a gunmetal gray dress that's tasteful in front, and practically obscene from the back. When she turns to exit the stage I can see two dimples between her hips, which means if her dress was a half inch lower in the back, the show would have to carry a PG 13 rating.

"God, she's gorgeous!" Lissie said.

"You think?"

"Don't you?"

I do. But what I say is, "Compared to you? Not so gorgeous."

A short time later I've got Lissie in bed. I'm really going after it, really hammering her.

I know I'm disgusting. I know she can't possibly want me touching her, much less riding her, but there she is, acting like I'm her version of Jinny Kidwell. Like I said, I don't deserve her.

I've got my eyes shut tight, mouth slightly open. My back arches upward…

Then something shifts in the cosmos.

I feel it beneath me.

One minute Lissie's into it, the next she's not.

Still, if I can just hold this image of Jinny in my mind for three more seconds...

But no.

Lissie says, "*Damn it* Buddy!"

And pushes me off.

"Jesus, Lissie! I was just about to—"

"I know *exactly* what you were about to do," she says, scooting away from me on the bed. I try to follow, but she makes her arm rigid between us, like Diana Ross, singing *Stop in the Name of Love.*

Then she says, "Who is she?"

"What?"

"Some new girl start at the office today?"

"What? Are you nuts? Of *course* not! Why would you even *think* that?"

She sits on the edge of the bed, her back to me. Her eyes follow the trail of clothes that runs from the door to her feet.

"Your friends were here today," she says. "What did you talk about?"

"Nothing."

"Nothing?"

"I swear!"

"Uh huh." She reaches down, picks her panties off the floor, slips them over her feet and pulls them to her knees. "Fine."

"Jesus, Lissie."

She stands, lifts her panties to her waist in a fluid motion, then goes to the dresser and selects a flannel nightie that practically screams, "Don't Touch Me!"

"Lissie, you're the only woman in my world. I swear!"

She shrugs the nightie on, walks back to the bed, and stares me down.

A moment passes before I cave.

"I mean, yeah, Richie and Mike are a little uncouth sometimes, you know? They were talking a little crude."

She waits. Like me, she's wondering where this is heading.

"I think maybe Mike likes you."

She arches an eyebrow. "What do you mean, *likes* me?"

I can't believe I'm willing to sell my friends out so easily.

"Well, he made a crack about how lucky I was to have you, and how you're way out of my league..."

I peek at her face to see if she's buying my bullshit. She isn't, but I have an endless supply and know how to shovel it.

I say, "I guess it hurt my feelings, you know?"

"Hurt your feelings."

"Yeah."

"Why?"

"Because I knew Mike was right." I shake my head. "It's true. I don't deserve you."

She gets a funny look in her eyes, like when her nephew soils his diaper, the one she just finished changing. She doesn't like changing diapers, but she loves her nephew.

"So this was some sort of caveman thing? Like I'm your woman or something?"

I shrug. "I guess."

Then her voice gets an edge to it and I know it's all going south on me.

"So you were going to show Mike who's boss."

"What? No!"

"No? Well, guess what: *this* time I believe you!"

"Uh...whaddya mean?"

"This had nothing to do with Mike, and your feelings weren't hurt. You were having sex with me, while thinking about someone else."

"I wasn't!"

"You were, and I won't *have* it!"

"What're you *talking* about? How can you even draw that conclusion?"

"All night at dinner you're staring at my body, not at *me*. Then you rip my clothes off, never once looking at my face. Then you start touching me differently, but still I give you the benefit of the doubt."

"Until?"

"Until just now."

"Ever dawn on you I might be adding variety to our love making?"

"Not when you pound me like a street whore."

"*What?*"

"You practically *raped* me! So don't even—"

She presses her lips into an angry frown and stares at me like I'm a stain in her panties.

Hoping to diffuse her anger with humor, I say, "I guess a blow job's out of the question?"

Lissie grits her teeth.

"Don't even *try* to tell me you weren't thinking about another woman. What's *really* going on? Are you having an affair?"

"No! Honey, I swear!"

She climbs back in bed and turns her back to me. "Thanks a lot, Buddy."

I put my hand on her shoulder. "Look, I—"

"Just...stop."

"But—"

"Real class act, you are."

"But—"

"Asshole."

Out loud I say, "Jesus, Lissie," but in my mind I'm thinking, *How did she know?*

But then I realize, women always know.

4.

IT'S THE MIDDLE of the night. Lissie's sleeping soundly.

I slide carefully out from under the covers, pad down the hall, and creep softly down the steps to the kitchen. I pour myself a glass of water, sit at the counter, open my laptop and fire it up. I feel guilty, like I'm sneaking porn or something. When the welcome bell chimes, I nearly jump out of my skin, and shuffle quickly to the hallway to look up the stairs to see if Lissie's coming. I stand there a full minute, but the house remains quiet, save for the light whooshing of my laptop fan in the next room.

I go back to the kitchen counter, click the internet icon and wait for the welcome page. When it appears, I type www.wishlist.bz in the address bar. A few seconds pass while I wonder what the hell .bz stands for, and then the survey appears, just like Mike said it would. I type in my email address, skip over the bullshit wording that gives the nut jobs hope that their wishes can come true, then type my list quickly:

Sex with Jinny Kidwell A million dollars My boss dies a horrible death I pause. The first three are bullshit; I know it, everyone knows it. But I allow myself to think, *what if*?

What if I put down something plausible? Maybe there's some whacko millionaire out there who's reading these lists, waiting for a sincere wish to pop up.

I think about it a full minute and finally decide to do

something special for Melissa, something to get her mind off what happened earlier. Wish number four becomes "Two Front Row Seats, Springsteen Concert, Louisville, Kentucky, Friday, March 12, 2010."

5.

THE NEXT MORNING Lissie's still upset. We barely speak while drinking our coffee. I apologize for the second time.

"You can't apologize for something until you admit doing it," she says.

Her eyes are pale blue, large, and full of disappointment. She looks down at her wheat toast and spreads honey on it.

Lissie works as a counter sales clerk in the makeup department of Macy's, nine to five, weekdays only, a schedule that allows us to spend quality time together every workday morning.

"I'm apologizing because I disrespected you last night."

She takes a bite of her toast and looks at me while chewing.

I add, "Instead of cherishing you."

She sighs. "Let's just get through the day."

"It was stupid," I say.

"Was it?"

"I was having a guy moment. I was being a jerk."

She studies my face with those giant doll eyes. Then, amazingly, she winks.

"Maybe tonight you'll get another chance. You know, to get it right."

I rush to her side and give her a hug. We're cheek to cheek, and her upper body is pressed against mine, and I think about Jinny Kidwell once again…

And realize I wouldn't trade Lissie for ten Jinny Kidwells.

Moments later I'm driving to work, a place where morale is so low you could shoot craps on it. My boss? What can I say—he's a client-stealing scumbag. I'm a loan officer at Midwestern Meadow Muffin's main office in downtown Louisville. That's not the actual name of the bank, but I don't want to be sued for slander. I'm on I-65, heading under the interstate, trying to merge into the right lane so I can make the Jefferson Street exit, thinking about how Boss Ogleshit threatened to fire me. Ogleshit isn't his real—oh hell, who gives a damn? I'm broke. Let them try to sue me! I work for Edward Oglethorpe, VP of Midwest Commercial Savings and Loan.

Friday, before closing, Oglethorpe said, "Buddy Flap-jack? I hope you've got another career lined up, because time's run out on this one. You've got one week to submit—" he looked at the printout in his hands—"three million in new loans. That's *new* loans, Buddy." To my coworker he said, "Marjorie Campbell? You're next in line. It's time to stop resting on your laurels, people. You're only as good as your last loan app."

I merge onto Jefferson Street and turn left into the bank's parking lot. I find a space, turn off the engine, and take a deep breath. If you've ever seen an abused dog cowering before its owner, that's me each day at the bank.

You need to realize—well, you don't need to realize anything at all. But I want you to know there are four loan officers here at the main branch, and we're all good at what we do. But every time we land a strong client, Oglethorpe swoops in, bribes them with golf dates, lunches, and sports tickets, and tells them to deal with him for future loans.

"What about Buddy?" my clients say.

"Buddy's a great guy," Oglethorpe says, "but he's a worker bee. If he writes your loan it has to go to committee for approval. That's fine for the average customer, but you're top tier, so why deal with subordinates? You need money, call me, personally. I can get you same day approval."

We can't compete with Ogleshit, so we've become hamsters on a wheel, always scrambling to replace the clients he steals.

As I enter the main office, all five senses are assaulted by the contrived atmosphere some bullshit artist conned the bank's management into buying. This is supposed to appeal to customers? Who says so? And who signs off on these decisions? Who approved the blue and black geometric-patterned carpet, the plastic potted plants and fake ivy clinging to the walls, the shiny wood veneer desktops, and mindnumbing Muzak piped through the ceiling speakers? Who selected the sickening sweet air freshener that squirts a blast of "Sunny Island Breeze" every fifteen minutes the first and third weeks of the month and "Polar Ice Mist" the second and fourth?

Muzak's upbeat version of "Tie a Yellow Ribbon" is playing, as it does every two hours of every day, as it has for the past six years, as it will for the rest of my career, which apparently means Friday. The cloying tune is half over, and I've been conditioned to know that "Please Release Me," is on deck. I wonder why companies like mine pay people to make bad music sound worse.

I pass Gus, the narcoleptic security guard, and head to my desk. Along the way, I nod in the general direction of the tellers'forlorn faces, but avoid making eye contact, since I can't abide their hapless glances.

I place my briefcase on my desk and take a seat in my faux leather executive desk chair. I close my eyes and take a deep breath, steeling myself for the beepy, electronic version of "Please Release Me" that's cuing up even as we speak. I open my eyes and flip the tabs on my briefcase to remove some papers, and feel a cold wave of evil wash over me. I look up and—

"Jesus!" I say, startled by the face that could launch a thousand shits.

Oglethorpe's secretary, Hilda, is standing over me, frowning, tapping her watch. My eyes instinctively go beyond her scowl to the faux wood clock on the wall. I'm five minutes early, which makes me ten minutes late, as per Oglethorpe's Fifth Rule of Success.

"Guess you don't care about office rules, since you're out of here on Friday," she says.

Bad as Ogleshit is, he's not the boss I wish would die.

Hilda is.

Since Ogleshit is out of the office most of the time, schmoozing my former power clients, Hilda has assumed control over the office. Everything that happens within the confines of that space is recorded in her journal: every remark, mistake, or profanity. Every water break, bathroom break, cough, giggle, or fart.

The bitch is relentless.

Last month, deep in an audit, I noticed it was 11:30 p.m. and realized I'd been working sixteen hours. I looked across the conference table at Hilda and said, "Wow, it's almost midnight."

Hilda's look told me I was dogshit on her shoe.

"I'm fading," I said.

"Sink or swim, Pancake," she said. "Your choice."

"Can I at least get some crackers, maybe take a quick cat nap?"

"Man up, Pancake. This ain't preschool, it's your job."

I manned up, kept my job.

When my grandmother was dying in the hospital, and the

rest of my family had gathered at her bedside, I asked Hilda if I could leave an hour early to share her final moments.

"You a surgeon?"

"No."

"Faith healer?"

"No."

"Not much you can do then."

"But she's dying!"

"Then let's remember her as she was, before the bad times. Wait a minute. Did she ever bake cookies for you?"

I nodded.

"Goody. Cling to that happy thought till closing time. But don't let it interfere with your work."

I know you think Hilda can't be this bad.

You're right.

She's worse.

6.

LUNCH. SECOND BEST part of the day, next to closing time.

Unless I'm entertaining a client, I only get forty-five minutes, so I have to make it count. I rush out the door, jump in my eight-year-old Taurus, and head for Tokyo Blue, where every Monday they offer a discount for those who sit at the sushi bar and order off a special menu. If I can get a seat at the bar, I'll have time to make lunch happen. If not, it's burger and fries, back at my desk.

The drive is four blocks to Broadway, two to Eighth, where a nearby parking lot provides easy access to the restaurant. Naturally, the lights are timed to make me stop at every intersection, which gives me plenty of time to think about the shameful way I'd spent the morning. I'd been forced by desperation to turn to the one thing I swore I'd never do: write letters to total strangers, invoking their children's affiliation with my niece, who attends Bluegrass Academy, the city's most prestigious private school.

I have two hours to change my mind, but the letters are already in the mail bag for the two o'clock run. I felt dirty signing my name to the sixteen dreadful letters, all of which had been personalized with information I extracted from my poor niece, Reece.

I wince thinking about the expression I'll see on Lissie's face tomorrow when her sister calls to tell her the disgusting way I'm pimping loans. Would she read one of the letters aloud to my wife? Of course she will:

Hi John and Beth,

My niece, Reece, told her Aunt Lissie and me how "awesome" your daughter, Meagan is. Apparently, our girls are quite the pair! Reece isn't ours, of course, but we get her on "loan" regularly. And that thought made me wonder if Meagan's parents are getting the best possible terms on their "loans."

On the chance you might benefit from the best loan rates in town, I'd like to call you Wednesday to see if we can meet on Thursday, so I can offer you a complimentary portfolio review.

Sincerely,

Charles 'Buddy'Pancake.

I know what you're thinking: could I possibly sink any lower? Stick around. You have no idea.

So sure, I hate myself. How could I not? But I loathe my job and my bosses even more.

How bad is my job? When I think about today's lone bright spot, this is what I come up with: I only have to hear "Tie a Yellow Ribbon" and "Please Release Me" two more times today.

Unless Hilda makes me stay till six-thirty.

In which case I'll kill myself.

7.

TOKYO BLUE IS filling up fast, but I spot three empty seats at the sushi bar. I claim the middle one, and within seconds a long-haired kid in a corduroy jacket and designer jeans grabs the one to my left. I can't help but notice the kid's Prada loafers and wonder how he managed to find employment that allows him to dress like this, and pays him well enough to afford it. I'm about to ask what he does for a living when I hear a voice to my right say, "What's good here?"

I turn my head to find the seat on my right occupied by an elderly lady wearing a hat that looks so ridiculous, people behind her are pointing and laughing. It's enormous, and beige, with a dozen huge, mudbrown feathers protruding a foot out the top, arranged in a circle, like some sort of aviary Stonehenge. I can't tear my eyes away from it, and wonder if maybe someone is filming the customers'uproarious reactions for a hidden camera TV show.

"What's good here?" she repeats.

"I'm sure it's all good," I say, slightly annoyed. I'm thinking about the whiz kid on my left, wondering if he's self-employed. Maybe he could use a line of credit to expand his business.

The elderly lady says, "What do *you* order?"

I frown. I'd hoped to have a quiet lunch, maybe fortify myself with a glass of sake to keep me from going back to work and cutting Hilda's head off. For a moment I think about stuffing her bloody, severed head in her panty hose like so much sausage, and smuggling it out of the bank. I picture her fat head bobbing up and down in the Ohio River current like a volleyball.

"I usually get the Derby Roll," I say. "It's got tempura shrimp in it. I don't usually go for the raw stuff."

She's watching the sushi chef pack a roll.

"Does he touch everyone's food with his hands like that?" she says, her voice much louder than necessary.

The sushi chef glares at her across the top of the glass bar, and I can only hope he doesn't think we're together. I look at his face and feel like hiding under my chair. She can't possibly comprehend the magnitude of the insult she's given him—suggesting he's unclean. I try to diffuse the tension before the old bat insults him again.

"What type of sushi do you normally like?" I ask.

"Never tried it. Nor will I, after watching Tokyo Joe put his hands all over the food like he's searching for a tumor."

"For the love of God!" says a young lady on the far side of the bar. She gives her ahi tuna a look of horror and lets it fall to her plate.

"Well, if you don't eat sushi..." I say to the old bat.

"I'm here for my granddaughter."

I don't understand. If she's here for her granddaughter, why is she sitting at the raw bar with me?

"Did she stand you up?"

Her face registers surprise. "Of course not! She's running late."

I nod. My interest lies only in the kid on my left, and who, if anyone, is handling his finances. But I can't seem to shut the lady up. I've become a conversation hostage.

"That's what they say nowadays," she says. "'Running

late.'" She picks up a plastic menu in her gloved hands and frowns. "What does 'running late' even mean? She's not running, she's just late."

The young man on my left finally looks up. A wave of recognition passes over his face.

"Mrs. Blankenship?"

She tilts her head up so she can peer at him through her bifocals.

"Do I know you, young man?"

He stands.

"Not personally, ma'am, but I help manage your AMCT."

"My what?"

"Ali Maddox Charitable Trust."

"That's Allison," she says, emphatically. "Not Ali."

"Yes, of course. I'm sorry. We often abbreviate, and shouldn't. My mistake."

Extending his hand to her he says, "I'm Rob Ketchel."

She nods. "I don't shake hands. Nothing personal, but you look like a scruffy vagabond to me. I suppose it's the style nowadays." To me she says, "I like the cut of your jib, though."

She turns her attention back to the menu.

Rob is uncomfortable standing there with his hand outstretched. He holds the pose a moment, then reclaims his seat.

"My granddaughter intends to hit me up for a loan," Mrs. Blankenship says. "You'd think she'd have the courtesy of meeting me at a decent restaurant and showing up on time."

My outlook brightens. "A loan, you say?"

8.

EVEN WITHOUT THE hat, Mrs. Blankenship is over-dressed for Tokyo Blue. She's wearing a tan linen skirt, white silk blouse, and a linen jacket that's too young and hip for her. The jewelry adorning her hands and wrists is the old fashioned, inherited kind.

It's finally coming together for me: Mrs. Blankenship. The Allison Maddox Charitable Trust. Sitting next to me, liking the cut of my jib, is none other than Whitney Blankenship, one of the wealthiest women in America.

I signal the waitress and clear my throat.

"I'll have a Derby Roll, and my lady friend will have a miso soup and salad."

Before Mrs. Blankenship can protest, I say, "My treat." Then I whisper, "They don't touch the soup or salad with their fingers."

She assesses me a moment, and says, "Well, why not? Serves my granddaughter right. I'll just start eating without her."

"An excellent lesson in punctuality," I say. Then add, "What type of loan is your granddaughter seeking?"

Mrs. Blankenship raises her eyebrows at my impudence.

"I'm only asking because I might be able to help. I'm a loan officer."

"For whom?"

"Midwest Commercial."

"Truly?"

"Would I lie to you?"

"I wouldn't know. You might."

"True. But why would I?"

She ponders this a moment, then says, "How's Jake?"

She's referring to Jackson "Jake" Robards, our President and CEO. Whitney Blankenship's eyes are dancing with humor. She's toying with me. Before I can respond she says, "When I wish to secure a loan from your bank I call Jake personally. Why on earth would I waste my time dealing with you?"

I hear Rob Ketchel's soft chuckle to my left. He's enjoying what he assumes will be the evisceration of my ego. But I've got an idea, an argument so brilliant and powerful, it seems divinely inspired.

"Mrs. Blankenship," I say. "Have you loaned money to your granddaughter in the past?"

"I don't see what business that is of yours."

"Bear with me, please. I'm trying to help. What's your granddaughter's name?"

"Chelsea."

"I'm going to assume that Chelsea is like a lot of grandchildren I've worked with, and if so, she's probably had a number of business ideas that haven't always been sound. I'm also going to assume that you're a loving grandparent who has loaned her money despite that fact. Or, at the very least, you cosigned her notes."

"Well of course I have. I love my granddaughter."

"But when we lend money for poor decisions, we're not teaching our youngsters sound financial practices, are we?"

"Are you suggesting I refuse to lend her the money?"

"Yes."

"Excuse me?"

"In a way."

She fixes a haughty gaze on me. "What's your intention here?"

"To protect your money, and help your granddaughter, Chelsea, become financially responsible."

"And?"

"And to convince you I'm the perfect person for this situation."

"You, and not Jake Robards."

"That's correct."

"And why is that?"

I smile. For once in my life I'm about to turn my biggest weakness as a loan officer into my biggest strength.

"My loans are required to go through committee for approval."

"Well, I don't see how that helps."

"If you send Chelsea to me, I can help her formulate a business plan that will have to be approved by our loan committee. If they don't like her idea, you'll have the perfect excuse to keep her out of your pocketbook."

She nods her head slowly. "And if they approve the loan?"

"They might lend Chelsea the money directly, and keep you out of it completely. Worst case scenario, you might have to guarantee the loan. But if they approve her loan, it's almost certain to be a good risk."

She thinks about it a moment, then smiles.

"What's your name, young man?"

"Buddy Pancake," I say, smiling broadly.

"You're joking," she says.

"Not in the slightest."

She laughs heartily. Then says, “How much is Mrs. Butterworth?”

I laugh lustily, as though I’d never heard such a witty remark in all my life. “What,” I say, “maybe five dollars?”

She howls with laughter.

9.

I MARCH INTO the office like a bullfighter with mustard on his sword.

"Howdy, Gus!" I holler.

I've startled him awake. He jerks to attention, grabs the butt of his gun before realizing I'm an employee on my way back from lunch.

I smile at the tellers. "Good afternoon, ladies!"

I walk over to the mailbag, turn it upside down on the mail desk and remove my sixteen shameful letters from the pile. Then I put the remaining letters back in the mail bag and look around the room. All eyes are studying me, just as they were on Friday when Oglethorpe threatened to can me. Only this time there's a nebbish curiosity in the air. I see Hilda pointing at her wrist watch, and I break into a loud song, effectively drowning out the Muzak. I'm performing both parts of Richard Wagner's *Tannhauser*, the Bugs Bunny and Elmer Fudd version:

"Oh, Bwoonhiwda you're so wuuuvwy!"

"Yes I know it, I can't heeelllp it!"

"Oh, Bwoonhiwda be my wuv!"

"For I wuuuuvvvvv youuuuuuu!"

I bow and hold my hands high in the air, expecting great applause.

The silence is deafening.

All faces turn to Hilda, whose mouth is hanging open like the door of a cargo plane. Suddenly she spins around, grabs her pen, and begins writing furiously in her notebook.

"Write all you want, you dreary shrew," I say, aware there are no customers on the floor. "But when you've completed your thought, write this down in your stupid journal and shove it up your big fat ass: I just landed the biggest account this bank has ever had!"

All afternoon I refuse to answer questions, saying only, "At nine o'clock tomorrow morning, you'll see. I'm going to *own* this bank!"

That evening, as I pull into my driveway, I see Lissie standing outside the front door holding an envelope in her hand. I stop and get out, wondering if it's a late payment notice. She runs to me and throws her arms around my neck.

"Lissie, what on earth?"

"I can't believe you did this for me!" she says.

"What?"

"Nothing says apology like front row seats to the Springsteen concert! How in the world did you manage this?"

My mind is going a hundred miles an hour. "Where did you get those?"

"The same way you sent them, my darling. Zip express! God, I could just eat you up!"

And a few minutes later, she did.

10.

"YOU'D BETTER GET going, rock star," Lissie says. "You're going to be late."

"No worries. I'm bulletproof."

It's Tuesday morning and I can't believe how fast my luck has changed. In an hour I'll be sitting with Chelsea Blankenship and her business associate, Emma Glendenning, who are applying for a million dollar line of credit for their new business. I don't know any of the details yet, but by the time I complete the loan app it will be a sure thing. Although Oglethorpe is demanding three million in new loans, Whitney Blankenship has promised to run all future Chelsea loans through me, which means my position at Midwest Meadow Muffin is cemented.

As if that's not enough, Lissie got her concert tickets last night, and I've become a hero in her eyes. I called it right, thinking some rich guy checking the Wish List website must have seen my request for tickets and made it come true.

Today at breakfast we're all smiles. She's talking about what she plans to wear to the concert on Friday.

"We better get moving," I say, "and quick!"

"Why the sudden rush? I thought you were bullet-proof."

I pointed at the window behind her.

"Check it out."

Across the street, two men in dark suits were knocking on

our neighbor's door.

Lissie laughed. "Jehovah's Witnesses? No problem, Glen and Barbara can handle them."

"Which means they'll be knocking on our door soon."

"Good point. Let's roll!"

Thirty minutes later I'm at my desk. Oglethorpe is watching me from his office door. You'd think he'd be thrilled that his branch is getting a big client, but no, he and Hilda are clearly upset. He's had all he can take. He strides to my desk and in his most demanding voice, says, "Who's your client?"

"You'll see."

"I could fire you before he arrives."

"Go ahead."

He's flustered. For the first time since I've known him, he can't intimidate me.

"Was there anything else?" I say.

"This better be good, Flapjack."

"Oh, it's good, Ogleshit."

"What did you call me?"

I'm about to repeat the insult in a loud voice so everyone in the office can enjoy it, but I suddenly hear a gasp from the desk beside me, and notice my coworker, Marjorie Campbell, isn't looking well. She's staring at the front door in horror. I follow her gaze. Two women have just entered the bank, wearing skimpy, skintight clothing. Their hair is wild and their makeup provocative. They appear to be hookers.

Hilda races across the floor.

"Oh no, you don't! Get out! *Out!* Gus?"

Gus awakes with a start, stumbles off his stool, grabs the butt of his gun, and looks around, surveying the situation.

One of the whores says something I can't hear. Hilda says, "Oh really?"

Then she starts cackling.

Oglethorpe says, "What's the meaning of this?"

Hilda shouts, "They're here to see Mr. Pancake about a business loan."

I jump to my feet and cross the floor to the women.

"Chelsea?"

"Hi, hon," she says. "This here's Emma Glendenning, my life partner."

I hustle them into the conference room, where I learn that Chelsea (five foot seven, bursting with tits) and Emma (braided armpit hair, pink spandex camel toe shorts, black and white prison-striped leggings) intend to start an online lesbian porn site with a twenty-four hour live camera feed covering every room in their house.

"*Every* room?" I say, as if that makes a difference.

"Of course!" Chelsea says. "Otherwise it wouldn't be an authentic portrayal."

"Of?"

"Of our lives."

I excuse myself and go to the employee wash room to splash some cold water on my face. I should flush myself down the toilet to catch up with my career, but instead I call the phone number Mrs. Blankenship gave me.

She answers, and I say, "Did Chelsea tell you what she and Emma plan to do with the loan proceeds?"

"I have a general idea, but I'd prefer not to hear the details. Why do you ask?"

"I mean, are you okay with this?"

"I have no control over her. Kids nowadays! It's all about fornication and sex tapes."

I rejoin the girls in the conference room, fill out the forms because I said I would, and escort them out of the building as surreptitiously as possible. Moments later Oglethorpe is reading my notes, laughing hysterically. He calls Hilda into his office and their conjoined laughter practically shakes the windows. Hilda opens the door and says, "Mr. Flapjack. If you would be so kind."

I enter Oglethorpe's office like my feet are made of lead. In less than a minute, it's over.

"Your contemptuous behavior toward Hilda yesterday, your deliberately profane pronunciation of my name today, and this joke of a loan application leave me no choice but to terminate your employment, effective immediately."

I'm thinking of future Chelsea Blankenship loans and wonder if I can convince him there is still value to be mined from the connection to Whitney Blankenship.

"Mr. Oglethorpe?"

"Shut up, Flapjack. Go clean out your desk. You've got ten minutes to gather your things. Then Gus will escort you to your car."

I turn to leave, but Oglethorpe's door is suddenly blocked by a lean, well-dressed businessman holding a manila folder in his left hand. He looks all business, and tough in a way that reminds me of a thirty-five year old Charles Bronson, with thick, black eyebrows and scrunched up facial features. His French cuffs are held in place with square-cut diamonds that, if real, appear to be at least four carats each. His left wrist sports a diamond-studded Piaget watch with a black alligator wrist band. The lines of the suit are unmistakable, though I've seen few of them in Louisville.

Bad as I feel, I can't help myself. I have to ask. "Is that a Brioni?"

"It is."

I nod, and start heading for my desk.

"May I help you?" Oglethorpe says, addressing the businessman.

"I'm looking for Buddy Pancake."

Stunned, I jerk my head around. Hilda, revealing her West End heritage, says, "He don't work here no more."

The businessman looks at Oglethorpe. "Is that true?"

"It is."

"Well that's a pity."

"How so?"

"I had hoped to apply for a twenty million dollar line of credit for my business."

"I can handle that for you!"

"Thanks, but I've been told to deal only with Mr. Pancake." He looks at me. "Are you he?"

I'm too stunned to speak.

"And you are?" Oglethorpe says.

The man presents his card with a practiced flourish.

My hopes are beginning to skyrocket.

But then Oglethorpe reads it and says, "Thomas Jefferson? That's very funny."

Thomas Jefferson nods as if he's accustomed to this type of response. Then he hands Oglethorpe the manila folder.

"My credit information. Let me know by noon on Friday if I might be of value to your bank. Assuming you reconsider employing Mr. Pancake."

Oglethorpe glances over the papers in the folder. He's a seasoned professional, adept at getting to the bottom line quickly. As he does so, his eyes grow wide as saucers.

"Do you mean to imply you're worth a quarter *billion* dollars?"

"I expect you to do a thorough check."

"Count on it, Mr. Jefferson. And if this is accurate?" He held the folder in his left hand and tapped it lightly with his right. "You don't need Mr. Pancake. You can deal with me directly, for instant approval."

"No offense, but I deal exclusively with Buddy Pancake. If on Friday he's no longer an employee of your bank I'll follow him to his next job."

I can't believe what's happening! An hour ago I thought the Blankenships would save my career, but they killed it. Now, this total stranger appears out of nowhere to save my job. I'm overwhelmed. I try to form the proper words to thank him, but when I clear my throat to speak, Mr. Jefferson holds up his hand.

"I'll require a loan application," he says.

Oglethorpe isn't convinced, but he isn't stupid, either. He allows me to fetch a loan app for Mr. Jefferson.

"Thanks, Buddy," he says. "I'll bring it back at noon, Friday." He starts to leave, then turns and hands me his business card, and says, "In the event you're no longer working here, take this to First City and tell Burt Jennings you've got my account. And Buddy?"

"Yes sir?"

"When you tell him your income requirements, give yourself a raise."

When Jefferson leaves, Oglethorpe tells me to stay at my desk until he is able to verify Thomas Jefferson's creditworthiness.

An hour later, a very sheepish Edward Oglethorpe calls me into his office and offers to reinstate me with full benefits and a modest raise.

I tell him I'll need to take a couple days off to consider his offer. I'll give him my decision by noon on Friday.

Then I blow him an air kiss and walk out the front door before his head explodes.

11.

IT'S FRIDAY MORNING, and all is right with the world. Lissie and I are in the kitchen again, having coffee.

"You think he'll show?"

"I do."

"Have you learned anything more about him?"

"Nothing more than I've told you."

After leaving the bank on Tuesday, I'd spent two hours researching Thomas Jefferson, of Simcoe, Jefferson Development. It had taken only minutes on the Internet to learn that Mr. Jefferson had recently announced his intentions to build a hotel and casino on the Ohio River to compete with the Horseshoe Southern Indiana gaming complex.

"Any idea how he got your name?"

"Best guess, Mrs. Blankenship recommended me."

"Did you ask her about it?"

"No."

"Why not?"

"I figured if she wanted me to know, she'd have told me."

"And she recommended you over every other loan officer in Louisville because?"

"You just want me to say it."

"I do."

"She likes the cut of my jib."

"Uh huh." Lissie takes a sip of coffee. I like what I see in her eyes these days when she looks at me. There had always been love, but now there's something else. Respect. Or maybe I respect myself more, and she's reflecting that.

"Tell me again about her hat."

I do, and she laughs.

"I still don't believe you about the hat," she says.

Wednesday and Thursday I attacked Lissie's "honey do" list of minor repairs I'd been putting off for the past year. I also got my car to the shop for the oil change and replacement tire I needed. With the raise I'd been promised, I bought a cable subscription and bonded with the allsports channel I'd coveted for years.

Lissie looks at her watch and says, "What time are you going in today?"

"Eleven should be late enough to make Oglethorpe sweat."

"Don't push him too far. He's been known to steal your clients before."

"I've got it covered."

"What time will you be home today?"

"No later than six. Why?"

"Are you kidding me?"

"Oh yeah. The concert."

"We need to leave by seven-thirty at the latest."

"No problem."

12.

IT'S TWELVE-THIRTY and I'm with Mr. Jefferson. In a limousine, not my office.

A half hour ago he entered the bank, handed Oglethorpe his loan application, and said, "Mr. Oglethorpe, if you have no objection, I plan to team up with Mr. Pancake for a round of golf against my partner, Ben Simcoe, and our CFO, Tony Blair."

"Tony Blair," he said. "Like the Prime Minister."

Jefferson nodded. "How long will it take to process my loan request?"

"Dealing as you are with Buddy, ten full days. Or we could bypass him and put you in play this very afternoon."

"Tempting," Jefferson said. "But I can wait."

Thomas Jefferson caught a ride with me to Louis Challa's Italian Restaurant, where we picked up panini sandwiches to go. Then the limo pulled up, so we left my car at the restaurant, and here we are.

Jefferson and I are the only passengers in the limo. There's a mini bar and TV on the right wall, and an outrageously long seat on the left that curves into a bench opposite us. For easy access, there's a third cabin door where that seat ends. From my vantage point I can see the back and side of the embroidered cap our driver is wearing.

A hundred "pin pricks" of fiber optic lighting in the ceiling switches from purple to blue, as does the plastic tube bordering the windows. When the blue turns to red, I cup the soft glove leather seat with my hand and wonder how long it takes rich people to get used to such opulence.

"Care for a bourbon?" Jefferson says.

"I'm good."

As we sit in silence, the light show changes from red to blue to green to yellow and back to the original purple. It's an impressive array, one I never knew existed, but one I'd grow tired of if I sat here long enough, much like the Muzak tape at the bank. Of course, while sitting in the limo, you don't have to look at the lights. You can look out the window as I'm doing now, watching us pass through the chain link gates of Glenwood Aviation. Now we're on the tarmac, slowly rolling toward a bright white Gulfstream jet, with burgundy striping.

Glenwood Aviation? Gulfstream jet?

"Where are you taking me?"

"Think about it."

I do, but nothing comes to mind.

"Did Mrs. Blankenship refer you to me?"

"Who?"

"Whitney Blankenship? The heiress? Richest family in Kentucky?"

He shrugs. "Oh, *that* Whitney Blankenship."

Seeing I'm alarmed, he adds, "Sorry, never had the pleasure."

"Then what the hell is going on here?"

The limo stops. The driver gets out and stands beside Jefferson's door. Jefferson turns to me and we lock eyes. "I'm going to level with you," he says. "We're not playing golf today."

"We're not?"

He shakes his head I look out the window and notice the jet's cabin door is open and the stairs have been lowered. A uniformed man who I assume is the copilot, stands quietly at the base of the stairs waiting.

Waiting for what?

I turn back to Jefferson.

"You think I'm gonna just hop on a jet with no idea where I'm going? I don't even *know* you!"

Jefferson sighs, but says nothing.

"Look, I appreciate what you've done for me, saving my job and all. But I can't go with you. My wife and I have plans tonight."

He dismisses my words with a wave of his hand. "You'll be back in plenty of time for the concert. In fact, you and Lissie will be riding to it in this very limo."

I do a double take. He knows about the concert? He knows my wife's name? I don't know what to say. I look at his steelgrey eyes and his diamond cuffs and think Jefferson may not be the scariest guy in the world, but he's certainly making me uncomfortable.

"Hannibal."

"Excuse me?"

"I'm taking you to Hannibal, Missouri."

"Hannibal."

"That's right. It's forty minutes there, forty back, and we'll be there two, two-and-a-half hours, max. We'll get you to Louis Challa's by five to retrieve your car, and you'll be home by five-thirty. Perkins will be in your driveway at six. You've got dinner reservations at Guiseppi's at six-fifteen, and from there, it's on to the concert."

"You must be joking! I can't afford all that!"

"The limo's on me. And by tonight, the cost of Guiseppi's

will be no more than an afterthought for you."

I roll my eyes. "Really? And why's that?"

"Because we're going to Hannibal!"

"So you say."

"Ready?"

"What the hell is in Hannibal?"

Jefferson taps the window with his knuckles, and Perkins opens his door. Before exiting the limo, Jefferson leans over to me and whispers, "Your million dollars!"

13.

WE'RE WHEELS UP in the jet, gaining altitude. The electronic map on the wall panel shows our speed, altitude, and estimated arrival time to Hannibal. I've just been told we're going there to pick up my million dollars.

From the wish list I filled out Sunday night.

"How is this possible?"

"You filled out the form," he says.

I'm exasperated, and the look on my face shows it. "You're trying to tell me that everyone who fills out a form gets their wishes?"

"No. Percentagewise, it's only a handful."

"Then, why me?"

"The wishes have to be grantable."

"But my list isn't possible."

"Why's that?" he says.

"The first item on my list was to fuck Jinny Kidwell."

Thomas Jefferson clenches his jaw.

14.

WE LAND AT Hannibal Regional Airport to find another stretch limo waiting for us. It's cold in Hannibal, and remnants of a recent snow line the runway. Jefferson and I climb into the car and ride a two-lane road a short distance until it intersects I-36. We take the eastbound ramp and pick up speed.

For the record, I don't believe we're on our way to pick up a million dollars in cash. At the same time, I'm not beyond considering the possibility, since in the past hour I've secured a twenty million dollar loan app and taken my first limo and private jet rides. I'm not sure what's going on, but I'm beyond thinking this is some sort of joke. I mean, why would anyone go to this much trouble for a joke? And if it *is* a joke, it's a helluva nice one! If this is someone's idea of funny, they can prank me every week!

"You're skeptical," Jefferson says.

"How could I not be?"

"Have I ever lied to you?"

"The golf game."

"I lied to Oglethorpe about the golf game. Not you."

I think he's splitting hairs, but I'm more interested in the money. "So you're saying I'm about to be a millionaire."

"That's what I'm saying."

"What's the catch?"

He seems surprised. "What makes you think there's a catch?"

"Well, according to the sign, we're already in Hannibal. You said we'll be here at least two hours. It shouldn't take that long to pick up a million dollars."

He studies me a moment, and says, "That's actually very perceptive. I may have underestimated you."

"So there *is* a catch."

"There is."

"I have to do something to get the money."

"Yes, you do."

"Something that's going to take me two hours."

A cloud passes over his face. I wonder if he's angry, or just sick of all my questions.

"That's up to you," he says.

"How long would it take *you* to do it?"

The look that may have been anger turns to sadness.

"A lifetime," he says.

We pass some farm houses, an antique barn, and a flea market whose sign says they're open weekends from April through September. I see billboards advertising Mark Twain's Riverboat Tour, and Cameron Cave, and a sign that shows which fast food restaurants are available at the next exit.

"This thing I have to do," I say.

"What about it?"

"Where is it going to take place?"

"Riverview Park."

"How far is that from here?"

"Couple minutes."

I feel a strong sense of foreboding. My stomach is poised to lurch. The only thing keeping me from vomiting is remembering Jefferson's comments: we're picking up the money, and we'll be back in Louisville by five. So whatever it is, it has to be something he feels I'm capable of doing. I ask myself, *what would I do for a million dollars?*

Would I do anything?

"I'm not going to kill anyone," I say.

"Darn!" he says, sarcastically.

We enter the park and immediately come to a guard station. Outside my window it looks like a police parking lot, with two dozen state and local cop cars, two sheriff's cars, and a dozen police motorcycles. None of the cops are with their vehicles, and all the lights are off. The driver shows his ID to the gate guy and we start moving slowly through the park, past an enormous yellow fire truck, two white ambulances, a red one, and three news vans with various station logos. There are taxis and tow trucks and cars of every style and color.

We're rolling purposefully through the park now, a park littered with tractor trailers, and sound and lighting systems. Two dark gray vans with *Department of Defense* emblems catch my eye, and then I see the people. Hundreds of them, clustered in groups. Some are having animated discussions, with cold air smoke billowing from their mouths. Others are milling around. We drive slowly through the mass of people, toward a line of giant trailers.

Standing before these five trailers, guarding them, are ten of the most formidable men I've ever seen. There are two such men in front of each trailer. They're wearing sunglasses and dark business suits and have electronic communication devices that extend from their ears to their mouths.

The limo pulls to a stop twenty feet in front of the largest trailer.

"What's in there?" I ask.

"Your money."

I look at the two guards standing between me and the trailer. Their dulleyed expressions suggest they could kill me faster than I could crush a grape.

I turn back to Jefferson.

"You're telling me there's a million dollars in that trailer?"

"That's what I'm telling you."

I focus on the trailer. It's about forty feet long, twelve high, with windowed sections pulled out on either side of the front door. It sits three feet off the ground, and is equipped with two propane tanks. Lettered on the lower right are the words *Elkhardt Location Equipment*, followed by a phone number with a 505 area code.

"A million dollars weighs less than you think," Jefferson says.

"Excuse me?"

"I'm just saying, you might be surprised by the weight."

"I work in a bank, remember?"

"You've held a million dollars in cash before?"

"Of course."

"Really?"

"Not all at the same time."

He nods. "That's funny." Then he adds, "A million dollars in hundred dollar bills weighs 20.4 pounds, not counting the weight of the straps around the bricks."

"Bricks?"

"Each brick is a $50,000 bundle. There are twenty bricks in a million dollars."

"I knew that."

"Of course, the briefcase will add some weight."

"Of course," I say, trying to sound as though I have these sorts of conversations every day.

We look at each other a moment.

"You swear to God there's a million dollars in that trailer, in a suitcase?"

He is either angry or impatient, and his face shows it.

"Briefcase," he says.

"Really?"

"Really."

I nod. "What do I have to do to get it?"

"Fuck Jinny Kidwell."

15.

THE ONE THING I know beyond all doubt is Jinny Kidwell is not in that trailer. Nor is there a million dollars in a briefcase in bricks of hundred dollar bills. But I also know I'm going to try to get past these guards and into the trailer, just to see how this thing plays out.

I take a deep breath, open the door, and approach the big eaters, fully expecting them to beat the living hell out of me. The first one holds me at bay with his ham hock of a hand while checking my face against a photo. After a few seconds, he passes it to the other guy, who studies it carefully, then says, "Your name?"

"Charles Pancake."

"Says here, Buddy Pancake."

"My nickname."

"Social Security number?"

I tell him.

He nods, indicating the trailer door. I walk up the aluminum steps and knock.

The first thing I notice about Jinny Kidwell is how tiny she is, and how frail she appears. The next is her porcelain skin. I'm so stunned to be in her presence, I nearly fall backward off the steps.

"Buddy?" she says.

I try to speak, but my throat is pinched shut. All that

emerges is a tiny mouselike squeak. I feel my face redden, and clear my throat to hide my embarrassment. She flashes her radiant smile, the one that earns the big bucks, and says, "Please come in."

I want to turn to see what's happening behind me, in case Jefferson and the body guards are laughing or getting ready to kill me or to see if I'm being filmed for some sort of cruel reality show. But my eyes are glued to her face. When she steps back and opens the door I enter. She closes the door, locks it, and briefly presses her body against it. Her back is to me, and her head dips slightly. She moves to the window and stops a moment to place her hand on the window pane. Her shoulders sag slightly, and I hear her give off a small sigh. Then she closes the curtains. When at last she turns to face me, her eyes appear moist, but her expression is incredibly seductive.

She glances to her right, and I follow her gaze to see a couch located in one of the sections that extends outward, that gives the front of the trailer a three dimensional look. In front of the couch is a small coffee table that holds a cutcrystal tumbler filled with ice.

"Can I pour you a drink?"

Jinny Kidwell said that. Not some look-alike actress, body double, or hightech hologram. Like Nicole Kidman, there is only one Jinny Kidwell, and her voice is as unique as her appearance. Often imitated by that talented comedian on *Saturday Night Live*, among others, no one can quite nail Jinny's voice. It's smoky like Demi Moore's, but not as husky or deep. So this is her, and we're in the same room, sharing the same air, and she's offered me a drink, and the only thing I can think to say is, "Why?"

Her laughter seems sincere. She takes a seat in the chair across from me and says, "Why, what?"

I gesture at her, and shake my head.

"Seriously, what's going on here?"

She starts to speak, then pauses, as if trying to formulate the proper words. While she does that, I allow my eyes to take in her entire frame. Although the Jinny Kidwell before me is very close to how she appears on the big screen, I realize the camera has never properly captured her perfect skin, upon which there are no blemishes, wrinkles, or marks of any kind. No freckles or moles on her face, arms or legs that I can see.

Speaking of her legs, they are jaw-droppingly perfect. Impossibly long, and toned to a degree that stops just short of being muscular, these legs draw you in and hold your gaze like Medusa's head.

"Are you okay?" she says.

I force my eyes upward. She's smiling coyly. What must her lips and tongue taste like? Before Lissie came into my life, all my sexual conquests smelled the same: like closing time at the local bar.

I put it all out there: "I'm old, fat, broke and ugly."

She smiled. "You're not so old."

"Compared to you, I'm a dinosaur. I'm a complete nobody. I'm lousy in bed, and…"

"And you're married," she says.

I'm stunned. "You knew?"

"You're married to Lissie. She's very pretty."

"You've *seen* her?"

"I've seen a photo."

I don't know what to say. Nothing makes sense.

"I'm married too," she says.

"You are?"

She looks at me curiously. "You sure you're a fan?"

"I know you through your movies."

She nods.

Despite the absurdity of my presence, I love being here, love knowing that Jinny Kidwell is sitting a mere six feet in front of me. I love her attention, love exchanging words with her, love looking at her.

But this is crazy.

"Jinny," I say, then shake my head thinking how ridiculous her name sounds coming out of my mouth.

She waits expectantly.

"Is it okay to call you Jinny?"

She looks at me as if I might be crazy. She's right. I'm in her trailer, been told I'm here to have sex with her, asking if I can call her by her name. I start over.

"Did they tell you why I'm here?"

She blushes.

I can't believe I'm sitting here talking to Jinny Kidwell, making her blush like a coed. She bites the corner of her bottom lip nervously.

And stands.

She's wearing—I now notice—a leopard print mini skirt and a black (she told me later) Ferretti silk tee, with a jeweled, sunburst print. I can't remember the style and pedigree of her sandals, but they were lovingly crafted by some premier designer exclusively for her.

She says, "Buddy, I don't know if I can make you understand this from my point of view, but in my whole life I've only been intimate with three men. I may seem like a household name to you, but the truth is I've only been a mega star for a year. Like you, I made a wish."

Every time she opens her mouth, I'm stunned by the words that emerge.

"You made a wish to be famous?"

She nods.

"And they somehow granted it?"

"They did."

"Who *are* these people?"

"I'll tell you this much: I've been given the opportunity of a lifetime, and it's good karma to give back. My wish was very important to me, and yours is very flattering."

"Flattering?"

"Yes."

"Why?"

"They told me your number one wish was to be intimate with me. Is that not true?"

"Yes, it's true, but—"

"—Out of every wish you could have made, this is the first thing that came to your mind. Can you not understand how amazing a compliment that is to me?"

"Yes, but—"

"But?"

"You're married," I say.

"As you are."

"Yes."

"And two hours from now, when you leave, we'll still be married."

I don't know how to respond to that, so I just stare at her mouth, wondering how the mere act of speaking can appear so provocative.

"Buddy?"

"Yes?"

She removes her blouse and says, "I want this to be a very special afternoon for you."

She's not wearing a bra.

"I'm not super experienced," she adds, "though to you I

probably seem wild on the screen."

Jinny Kidwell is standing in front of me, and she's not wearing a bra.

She reaches behind her with both hands and I hear the sound of a zipper lowering. She does a sort of hip shake and her skirt slides to the floor, and...

...She's not wearing panties.

She says, "All I ask is that you treat me with respect."

"Huh?"

"With respect."

"Okay."

"And don't do anything to hurt me."

"Hurt you?"

She blushes again.

Then I blush.

16.

IF I COULD have a fifth wish it might be that I'm the most amazing lover Jinny Kidwell has ever encountered.

But the truth is I'm unable to perform.

"This has never happened to me," I say.

"Nor to me," she says.

"I can't do this to Lissie."

"I believe you."

"No, I mean—"

"I know what you mean, Buddy. I was just kidding."

"Oh. Right."

We're sitting on her bed, and we're both looking at the pathetic, drooping thing between my legs I used to call my "mighty sword."

"He looks tired," she says.

I wince.

"What's the problem, do you think?"

I shrug. "I think maybe I'm just overwhelmed."

She nods. Then, as if trying to enhance my mortification, she reaches over and pokes it with her finger. Then she lifts it with her thumb and index finger, holds it aloft a second, then lets it fall, and I want to crawl in a hole somewhere.

She frowns. "So what's the plan, Stan?"

"Excuse me?"

"We've got to get this thing done. What do you suggest?"

I've never had a woman stare at my manhood as if it were a snail on a plate. Nor have I ever had a conversation with anyone about it, while staring at it. I sigh. "Maybe we should just forget the whole thing."

A sudden look of fear enters her eyes.

"It doesn't work that way," she says. "We have to do this."

She starts breathing rapidly, as if she might hyper-ventilate. I reach out and place my hand on her shoulder.

"Hey, relax," I say. "I can tell them we did it. No harm, no foul."

She shook her head. "You don't understand. I made an agreement. You have to perform!"

I look at my lap and mentally curse my dick.

Jinny says, "Give me a sec."

She leaves the room a minute and comes back with a small bottle of water and a pill.

"Here," she says, "take this."

"What is it, Viagra?"

"No."

I stare at the little pill in my hand. "Is it safe?"

"One is safe. Six is an addiction."

"Will it help me perform?"

"It won't hurt."

I look into her gorgeous eyes. "Are you in some kind of trouble?"

"Please, just take the pill."

I swallow it and set the glass down.

"Now what happens?" I say.

"You lie down and relax. I'll turn on some music and we'll see what happens."

"Sounds good."

Some time must have passed. I'm not aware of any time

passing, but something must have happened, because I'm suddenly aware that Jinny Kidwell is bitch slapping me and calling me names.

No, wait. That's not what happened.

I shake my head, trying to clear the cobwebs. I now realize she slapped me once, lightly, and said, "Focus, Buddy!"

"What happened?"

"You're back!"

"How long was I out?"

"A couple minutes."

"Sorry."

"That's okay. Hey, I have an idea!" Jinny says, brightly. "Have you ever acted before?"

"What, like in a play?"

"Uh huh."

"Not really."

"Well let me put a thought in your mind."

"Okay."

"You know I have love scenes with actors in my movies, right?"

"Uh huh."

"Well, *I* know I'm married, and the actors know *they're* married, but the way we get the public to believe our scenes is to pretend we're *not* married."

"That makes sense."

"It does. And here's the thing: Lissie doesn't know you're here. In two hours our lives will go back to what they were before we met. Lissie won't know what we've done, and she'd never believe it anyway."

"That's certainly true."

"I'm giving you a gift, Buddy. The most special gift I can give a man."

I nod.

"And there's something else," she said.

"What's that?"

"We've already seen each other naked, so the rest isn't such a big deal."

I look at her nakedness some more.

"I've got another idea," she says.

I wait to hear it.

"I think it might help if I show you a view of my body that's never been filmed."

And she does.

Two minutes later, meaning our entire romantic encounter lasted maybe half that long—we talk about making movies, and the type of blouse and sandals she'd been wearing, and how hard it is to be her, with cameras in her face and people shouting and pushing every time she turns around. As she talks, her breasts rise and fall and I become swept up in her delicate beauty and—bless her heart—she allows me a mulligan, and this time I'm playing from the championship tees!

As our second hour comes to a close I feel as though I've known her all my life. We're lying on her bed, gazing into each other's eyes and she seems as if she's about to cry.

"I'm so sorry," she says.

"Sorry? About what?"

"What I've done."

"You mean the pill?"

She places her palm on my cheek. "You're a really nice guy, Buddy. I'm just...It's..."

Suddenly she says, "Oh my God! I almost forgot!"

She slides off the bed and heads to her closet. It's the first time I see her standing with her back to me, and she looks like a different person. She's extremely frail from this angle. Her backbone protrudes like a Rhodesian Ridgeback's. I'd seen her entire back from a distance on the Academy Awards show, but here, in person, it seemed to belong to a different person. She stumbles and nearly falls into the wall. I sit up, preparing to rush over to help her in case she's about to faint, but she regains her footing and steadies herself against the doorway of her closet.

"Are you okay?" I ask.

She laughs. "I'm terribly clumsy. Promise you won't tell!"

Her breathing seems shallow and irregular and I wonder if it had been this way the whole time and I simply hadn't noticed till now, having been so caught up in the experience.

"There it is," she says, and takes a couple of steps into her closet. She bends over and picks up a briefcase, and brings it back to me.

"Your money," she says.

17.

I'M IN THE limo with Thomas Jefferson, heading back to the airport. He's tapping his fingers.

"She paid me the million dollars out of her own money?"

"It appears she did," he says.

We sit without speaking. The tapping grows louder as Jefferson seems totally consumed by the challenge of moving his fingers faster and faster against the armrest. He's preoccupied, fidgety, and very possibly angry, which seems completely out of character for the smooth, confident businessman I'd met in the bank.

"Is something wrong?" I say.

"*Is something wrong?*" he mimics, derisively.

"Is there?"

He stops tapping his fingers and gives me a hard stare. "Was she a good fuck?"

He practically spat the words at me. I'm shocked by his demeanor, which has turned confrontational. I'm trying to decide if Thomas Jefferson is jealous, unstable, or both.

"It wasn't like that," I say.

"Care to enlighten me?"

"You wouldn't understand."

"Try me."

"It was..."

I look at Jefferson's face. He seems to be fighting to keep

his anger in check. He repeats my words: "It was...what?"

"It was...like magic."

The anger leaks out of him slowly, like a balloon with a small nick in it. His lips press together in a flat line. "Well, how nice for you."

I nod. "But why would she give me a million dollars?"

"What did she say?"

"Something about paying back into the system that helped her become a star."

"Makes sense."

"Who *are* you guys?"

"Who indeed?" he says, with a heavy sigh.

He closes his eyes and doesn't speak again until we're on the tarmac. As the limo pulls to a stop near the jet he says, "You need to use the restroom before we take off?"

"No, I'm good."

"Then, let's get you back to your car."

It's a quiet flight back to Louisville. When the jet comes to a stop, I remain seated so Jefferson can get out first, but he makes no effort to move. Instead, he gestures at the briefcase in my lap. "You get it all counted?"

He's referring to the way I opened and closed the briefcase several times during the flight, picking up one brick after another, riffling through them.

"You think the money's real?" I say.

"I guarantee it. Everything about the Wish List experience is real. Except that I'm going to decline the twenty million dollar loan."

"Why?"

"You'll know soon enough."

I pat the briefcase and laugh. "In that case, how long do you think it'll take me to quit my job on Monday?"

"I doubt you'll do much thinking about the bank from here on out."

"Why's that?"

Instead of answering, he says, "Does it even bother you that an hour ago you were with another woman, and now you're heading home to face your loving wife, pretending you've been hard at work all afternoon?"

His words don't hit me as hard as he probably thinks they should. Yes, technically, I cheated on my wife. But it's not as though I deliberately set out to cheat. In fact, it was Jinny who talked me into actually doing it. And there's this: I'm holding a million dollars in cash on my lap!

I respond by saying, "How many guys on the planet do you know who'd refuse a million dollars to have sex with Jinny Kidwell?"

Jefferson shakes his head. "You have no clue, do you?"

The way he said it gives me pause, and I wonder again if he's jealous, or simply trying to rain on my parade.

"What do you mean?"

"Ever heard the expression 'there's no free lunch?'"

"Look, this isn't some huge moral issue. It's not like I'm having an affair. This was a onetime opportunity that will never be repeated. In any event, there's no way Lissie will find out about Jinny. And even if she did, she'd never believe it."

"So, if the positions were reversed, Lissie would have slept with a movie star?"

This time his words take a bite out of my heart. I hang my head. "No, she wouldn't have done it, even for a million dollars."

"So how does that make you feel?"

"How does that make me *feel*? Well, hey, now that you've brought it up, it makes me feel like shit. So, thanks for that.

But I've always known Lissie was a better person than me."

"Meaning?"

"Should a lesser person be held to the same standard as a better one?"

There's no way he can hide his contempt. But I stand behind my belief that few men on earth would have turned down an afternoon delight with Jinny Kidwell, with or without the money.

He says, "You haven't read the fine print, have you?"

"What fine print?"

"No one ever reads the fine print," he says, as if to himself.

"What fine print?"

"On the website. Wishlist.bz."

I think about Sunday night, when I accessed the website. I'd been rushing, worried Lissie might walk in on me.

"There was no fine print," I say, aware there's little confidence in my voice.

"You can't type in your wishes until you click the box and agree to the terms."

He can tell by the expression on my face that I remember clicking the little box.

"What terms?" I ask.

He leans his head back against the headrest and closes his eyes.

"What's in the Agreement?" I ask.

I notice his fingers have started tapping again. When he speaks, it's just two words:

"Your life."

I leave Thomas Jefferson in the jet, thank the pilots for the flight, and walk down the steps toward the limousine. Perkins holds the door open for me, and I slide into the car and notice a guy sitting across from me.

A guy who looks like a gangster.

When he eyes my briefcase, I put both arms around it and hug it tight against my body.

"Who are you?" I say.

"Your worst nightmare."

18.

"HERE'S HOW IT'S going down," he says. "We're going to drop you off at your car, and you're going to drive straight home, observing the speed limit, and when you get there, you're going to lock your car in the garage. Then you're going to enjoy a funfilled evening with your wife."

"Sounds good so far," I say, trying to give the impression I'm not the least bit afraid of him.

"After the concert you're going to put the wife to bed and you're going to meet me and another guy in your garage."

"And why would I want to do that?"

"Because I got a job for you."

"Not interested. I'm retired."

"This is nonnegotiable."

"What's that supposed to mean?"

"It means it's time to start paying back."

"For what?"

"The wishes you received."

"No one said anything about paying for the wishes."

"And yet here we are."

"Just for the sake of argument, what sort of payment are we talking about?"

"You're going to bury a body."

"Excuse me?"

"Remember wish number three?"

My boss dies a horrible death.

"Bullshit."

He puts his hand in his suit jacket, removes a photograph, hands it to me. It's my boss, Edward Oglethorpe, with a bullet hole between his eyes. I've never seen a dead body before, except my grandmother's, and she didn't have a bullet hole in her head.

"This could be a fake," I say.

"You'll have a chance to see for yourself soon enough."

"Why's that?"

"I already told you: you're going to bury him tonight."

"I don't believe you."

"Do you have front row seats to Springsteen tonight? Did you fuck Jinny Kidwell today? Are you holding a briefcase with a million dollars in it? I were you, I'd believe it."

The thing is, I *do* believe it. But I'm busy trying not to be sick. The contents of my stomach are swirling, and there's a weird ringing in my ears.

"You killed my boss?"

"No, *you* killed him. By wishing it."

"But...I was just kidding around! I didn't expect someone to actually *kill* him!"

"Oh, really? Gee, you should have said."

"You're mocking me."

"You think?"

"What if I refuse?"

He smiles a fierce, terrifying smile. "There's no refusing. Ask Pete."

"Who's Pete?"

"The guy you been with since noon."

"You mean Thomas Jefferson?"

"Oh, and *that* didn't give you a clue?"

"That's not his name?"

"Try Pete Rossman."

"I don't believe you. Jefferson's paperwork checked out. I *Googled* the guy, for Chrissakes!"

"Oh, well, if you *Googled* him."

"You're saying Thomas Jefferson, or Pete Rossman, or whatever his name is—doesn't work for you?"

"Yes and no."

"What's that supposed to mean?"

"He's in it the same way as you."

"I don't understand."

"Pete Rossman. Name doesn't ring a bell?"

"No. What's his claim to fame?"

"Pete's a wealthy businessman, likes to keep a low profile. He's hardly ever seen in public."

"So?"

"His wife, on the other hand, is quite well known."

"Who's his wife?"

"Jinny Kidwell."

19.

THOUGH MY CAR is parked near the entrance to Louis Challa's, the limo pulls to a stop some fifty feet away. We're at the far corner of the parking lot, facing the second curb cut.

"Your cell phone no longer works," he says. "And we've tapped your home phone. Your computer, too."

"Why?"

"We're a controlling bunch, at least until we get what we want."

I don't like the sound of that. Up to now, I've been waiting for Perkins to open my door, but he's still in the front seat, probably scared to move without being told. I shrug and let myself out the door and fish the keys from my pocket. I've got the briefcase in my left hand, but it's feeling ten times heavier than the last time I lifted it. My head is reeling. Why would Rossman set up a line of credit in a phony name and fly me all the way to Hannibal to have sex with his wife? And why would he let her give me a million dollars for the privilege? The whole thing is completely insane.

I lean my head back in the limo and say, "I never caught your name."

"Pete and Jinny call me Rudy."

"Why would Rossman let me have sex with his wife?"

"That's their business."

"Fine, don't tell me. I already know."

He rolls his eyes in an exaggerated manner, like a teenage girl being lectured by her father. "I sincerely doubt that."

"Somehow you guys turned Jinny Kidwell into a mega star. She's paying you back by granting my wish."

He laughs. It starts as a chuckle, but keeps building. It isn't a fake laugh. Finally he says, "Pete said that?"

"Jinny told me," I say, indignantly.

"Yeah? Well, she lied."

"I don't think so."

"What, two hours in the sack, you think you know her character?"

"Yeah, that's right."

"I hate to burst your bubble, Chachi, but she's an actress, remember?"

"If Jinny lied, then what's the real wish you granted her?"

"Maybe she put fucking you at the top of *her* list."

"Right. Look, I'm serious. What was Jinny's wish?"

"It's not my job to tell you."

"And just what *is* your job, Rudy?"

His eyebrows arch, but his voice remains even. "Collecting payments."

"Payments for what?"

"The wishes you get."

I'm standing in Louis Challa's restaurant parking lot, leaning into a limo, talking to a guy who is as far from a fairy godmother as a choirboy is to a congressman. There are people milling about the parking lot, so I straighten up and look around to make sure no one can hear our absurd conversation.

I lean my head back in the car and ask Rudy, "What did you do to her?"

"Who?"

"Jinny. To make her have sex with me."

"It's not like you think. I don't force people to do a certain thing."

"You don't?"

"No."

"You're telling me Jinny didn't *have* to sleep with me? She *chose* to?"

"Yeah, more like that. See, I give people two choices, sometimes three. We try to be accommodating."

"And of all the choices you gave Jinny, having sex with me was the least objectionable?"

He made a gun out of his thumb and index finger, pointed at me, and pretended to shoot.

"So she's paid up?" I say.

"Her payment has four parts."

"Sleeping with me was one, right? She paid me a million dollars, that's two. What are the other two?"

"That's between her and us."

"She's rich, so the money was no big deal. Sleeping with me probably wasn't *that* huge of a sacrifice…"

"Says you. But remember, her husband had to sit in the car and wait while she had sex with you. Can you imagine how hard that must have been for him?"

No. I couldn't imagine it. Didn't want to, didn't try to imagine it.

"So that was her third thing?"

"No. That was one of *his* things."

"Holy shit!"

"Exactly."

"Am I involved in her other repayments?"

He shrugs.

"When will you tell me? After I help you bury the body?"

Rudy gestures at the open air around me. “I wouldn’t speak so loud, if I were you.”

I look around again, but no one is within hearing distance.

“Are you riding home with me?”

“No. Perkins will drop me off before picking you guys up for dinner.”

“How do you know I won’t drive straight to the cops?”

“It wouldn’t be prudent.”

“Why’s that?”

“There’s a dead body in your trunk.”

20.

I LOOK AT my car. I want to run to it, open the trunk and prove him a liar. But customers have started arriving at the restaurant, and I can't take the chance someone might see. Then I think of something.

"The car keys," I say, holding them up, jingling them in my hand.

"What about them?"

I show him a smug smile. "You couldn't have put anything in my trunk. I had the keys with me the whole time."

He reaches into his pants pocket and tosses me a set of keys on a key ring that looks exactly like mine. I hold them next to each other, starting with my car key.

Identical.

I try my house key.

Identical.

My office key.

Identical.

"Where did you get these?"

"You'd better get moving. Don't want to be late for the concert."

"You've been inside my *house*?"

"I'll see you later tonight, in your garage. One a.m. Don't be late."

"What if I refuse? You can't just make me bury a body."

"Climb back in a minute, and close the door." He sees the look on my face and adds, "Relax, we're just going to have a little chat."

I do as he says. When I'm settled in, he says, "I didn't kill your boss."

"What?"

"I didn't kill Oglethorpe."

"So what, this was all a joke?"

"No, he's dead. It's just that I didn't kill him."

"Who did?"

"A housewife from New Albany."

"Indiana?"

"Yeah."

"Why?"

"She wanted to commit a perfect crime."

"She wished it?"

"There's a guy from Kansas City, name of Jansen. You don't wanna know his first name, trust me. Guy's a sick degenerate, violent, done some prison time at ADX."

"What's that?"

"Toughest prison in America. Anyway, we're in the middle of granting his wishes."

"So?"

"He wants to barbecue a living man, and eat him."

I can't see my face, but I'm sure he can tell I'm concerned. He continues: "We've already picked out a victim for him, a homeless guy in St. Louis. But we can easily make it you."

I'm shuddering as I speak, so my voice comes out weird, and stuttering: "A-a-all I've g-g-got to do is b-bury a b-body?"

"Yeah, that's all," he says. Then adds, "For now."

21.

LISSIE'S ENJOYING THE dinner more than me.

I'm trying to make it a special night, but all I can think about is the fine print and what I have to do in a few hours. I keep looking around the restaurant for Rudy, or Pete Rossman, or even Perkins, the limo driver. But if anyone's watching us, it's no one I know. Hell, maybe it's everyone in the room. For all I know, there could be hundreds of people involved. If the fine folks at Wish List can grant all these wishes and force people like Rossman and Jinny Kidwell to participate, they must be incredibly well-funded and staffed.

They might be invincible.

"Cheers," Lissie says, clinking my glass with hers. "This is amazing! Dinner at Guiseppi's, the limo, the concert…tell me the truth: how big was the raise?"

"Huge."

Her eyes are sparkling. "I'm so proud of you!"

"Thanks."

"No, seriously, Buddy, this is a dream come true. After all this time, you've finally made it!"

I wonder if I've made it. Specifically, I wonder if the hundred dollar bills in my pocket are counterfeit.

They're not, I learn, after paying the bill.

Much as I dread the idea of burying my boss in a few hours, I like giving my beautiful wife a well-deserved night on the town, and watching her eyes light up when I pay the tab with hundred dollar bills. I like the way I've suddenly become more powerful in her eyes, proving the adage that nothing hides a man's flaws like success.

In the limo, after the concert, her hands are all over me. She wants to put up the partition, but earlier, when I went to meet Perkins in our driveway to tell him Lissie was running a few minutes late, he'd said, "No hanky panky in the limo tonight," so I tell Lissie she'll have to ravage me when we get home.

"Don't think I won't," she says.

We pull up in the driveway and Perkins lets us out, saying, "Lissie, it's been a pleasure. Might I escort you to the door?"

Tipsy, giggly and adorable, she turns to me and tries to adopt a dignified, snobbish accent: "Perkins wishes to escort me to our abode, Charles. Does that meet with your approval?"

Perkins signals me to stay behind. "Of course, dahling," I say, attempting to match her accent. "Go on in. I'll settle up with the good man and join you momentarily."

They walk to the front door and Perkins waits for her to enter. As she does, Lissie gushes, "Perkins, this has been the most wonderful night ever. Thank you for driving us. It's been such a pleasure to meet you!"

"The pleasure's all mine, Miss."

She looks at me, standing by the car. "I've got the greatest husband in the whole world! What do you think, Perkins? Is he a keeper?"

"He's certainly one of a kind, Miss."

Perkins watches her enter the house and close the door. Then he approaches me.

"You think I'm scum, don't you?" I say.

"We're all scum," he says. Then he points at the front door. "Except for her. A girl like that? She deserves better."

"What happens now?"

He reaches into his pocket and removes a white capsule and hands it to me. "You're going to pull the capsule apart and empty the contents into her drink. You're going to stand over her and make sure she drinks every last drop."

"What is it?"

"A sedative."

"Is it safe?"

"Of course it's safe. A word to the wise, make sure she's in bed when you give it to her."

"Why's that?"

"Look, you're running out of time, so don't screw this up, okay? No long-winded toasts, no love talk, no sex. Get this into her system immediately. You do that, she'll be zonked by one o'clock, and she'll stay that way until you return."

"You going to be here when Rudy comes?"

"No."

"He said there'd be another guy here."

"So?"

"You know who it is?"

"No."

"You seem a nice guy, Perkins. Why are you involved with a guy like Rudy?"

He pauses a moment, then says, "Buddy, look at me."

I look into his impassive face.

"Yeah?"

"Don't make the mistake of thinking you and I are friends, because we're not. Personally, I don't give a shit what happens to you."

"Okay. It just seemed like you were trying to help."

He gestures to the house. "Her, not you."

"Story of my life," I say.

"She deserves better."

I can't argue the point, so I look at the capsule in my hand, and say, "Lissie doesn't really drink at home."

"You better hope she does tonight."

"Why's that?"

"If she's awake, Rudy will make her participate."

22.

LISSIE SAYS SHE'LL be happy to toast to our new success after slipping into something more comfortable, which turns out to be a sexy nightie she'd purchased for the occasion.

"You like it?"

"Love it!"

We're in the bedroom. I'm sitting on the edge of the bed, holding two glasses of wine. She's standing in front of me, lifting the nightie, offering me a peek at her matching see-through panties.

"Wanna test drive?"

I do, but I remember what Perkins said about getting the drug into her system immediately. He made a good point about not giving Rudy an excuse to involve Lissie in the whole Jinny Kidwell and Ed Oglethorpe situations. Jinny said Lissie would never believe what we did, but Rudy strikes me as the type of guy who'd have proof. Lissie might also wonder what type of monster could escort her to dinner and a concert while knowing he had a dead body in the trunk of his car the whole time.

It takes some urging, but I finally get her to sit beside me and drain her glass. Perkins was right about making sure she was in bed first, because the minute I get our empty glasses on the night stand, Lissie falls sideways and slides off the bed. Fortunately, I'm within three feet of her, so I'm able to catch her before she hits the floor. She seems twice as heavy as she should, and I remember reading a novel once about how carrying "dead weight" is much harder than people think.

In any event, I manage to get her on the bed, and push her far enough toward the middle to keep her from rolling off again. She's snoring lightly, so I put a pillow under her head and turn her sideways. I kiss her cheek and change into some clothes I hope are appropriate for burying a body.

According to my watch, I've got about twenty minutes. I wonder if I should have another drink, to fortify myself for the grave digging, but decide that between what I consumed at dinner, and the wine just now, I've had enough. I turn out the bedroom lights and stand by the window that faces the front yard. I'm worried about the meeting for several reasons. One, Rudy scares the shit out of me. Two, though it's hard to imagine, the guy Rudy's bringing might be worse. Three, what if I get caught? Four, poor Mr. Oglethorpe. Sure, he was a bastard of a boss, but he has a wife and kids who probably care for him. Now he's dead, and for no better reason than I wished it—and I wasn't even referring to him in the first place! If anyone from work should die a horrible death, it's Hilda. Five, digging a grave is bound to be strenuous work. I wonder how long it's going to take. Six, I wonder if maybe the grave I'm digging is really for me. I never saw Oglethorpe's body in my trunk. I wanted to open the trunk and look when I got home, but I also wanted to hide my money in the garage, and jump in the shower before Lissie could pick up Jinny's scent on me.

I turn to look at my wife. If the grave is for me, I'll never see her again, and she'll never know what happened to me. I wonder if I should leave a note of some kind. Then decide that's a terrible idea. If they can grant impossible wishes they can certainly destroy Lissie's life. I wonder if they'll let her keep the money after I'm dead. It seems the decent thing to do, if they're going to kill me. I wonder how long it will take her to find it.

I can't leave her a note saying there's money hidden in the garage. Knowing Lissie, she'd report it to the cops. I don't know what to do about the money right now, so I decide to do nothing, except hope they won't kill me.

I'm still standing there, looking out the window, thinking I should bring another set of clothes and sneakers, so I can change afterward. It wouldn't be smart to drag dirt from the crime scene back into the house in the event something goes wrong.

Jesus, listen to me: crime scene!

I'm in way over my head.

It's dark outside, but there's a streetlight on the corner that offers enough light for me to make out the forms of two people dressed in black, emerging from Bill and Norma's back yard. I watch them cross the street and walk down my driveway. The river of ice in my veins makes it hard for me to move, but I force my way out of the bedroom and close the door carefully, praying Lissie sleeps peacefully until my return. I get down the stairs as quietly as possible, and enter the garage, making sure to lock the door that leads from the garage to the house before acknowledging the two men who have just entered my garage.

The first one to get his mask off is Rudy. But you could have knocked me over with a feather when I see who the other guy is.

23.

"WHAT THE HELL?"

The guy standing beside Rudy is Richie, my best friend in the world, with the possible exception of Mike. Richie's usually pretty lively, but tonight he looks like he's carrying the weight of the world on his shoulders.

"What's going on here?" I ask.

Richie turns away, and Rudy motions me to be quiet. "Buddy, you're driving. Richie, shotgun. I'm in the back. Let's go."

I fire up the car and ease out my driveway before switching on the headlights. As Rudy directs me where to go, I try to make eye contact with Richie. But he's looking out the passenger window.

"Where are you taking us?" I ask.

"Shut up."

We take I-71 toward Cincinnati about thirty miles and get off at Exit 31. We bypass the small town of Talmadge, and work our way deep into the countryside. After passing a dozen nondescript dirt roads, Rudy says, "Turn left at the next one."

"Are you planning to kill us?" I say.

"Yes."

"What?"

"If you keep talking, I will. Jesus, do you ever shut up?"

I turn where he said to, and we're in the middle of a hay

field that's taller than our car. The road is nothing more than two tire tracks heading God knows where.

Throughout the trip, Richie has said nothing, hasn't even looked in my direction. A chilling thought strikes me.

I push his arm to get his attention. "Richie, are you in this with Rudy?"

Rudy's fist crashes into the back of my head, causing me to jerk the car off the road, into the hay field. The tires are spinning, fighting for traction.

Rudy says, "I told you to shut up, asshole. Now get back on the road, or I'll make the next punch hurt."

Was he kidding me? The first punch hurt like hell! I wouldn't be able to handle a harder one. My eyes are crossed so badly I can barely get back on the tire tracks. Once there, I keep drifting to the right. Each time I do, Rudy cuffs the side of my head to get me back on course.

He guides me to a thick stand of bushes and trees and tells me to put the car in park and surrender the keys. I do, and he pops the trunk and tells us to get out. Now Rudy's holding a flashlight, which he uses to motion us behind the car. Once there, he comes up behind us and points the flashlight into the trunk, and we see a thick, black plastic bag with a thick seam of sealing tape around the center. He's put one bag over the torso, the other over the feet, and taped them together in the middle.

"You want to open it to make sure it's him?"

"No, I'm good."

Rudy chuckles. "All right, one of you on each end. Lift him out and let's go."

Richie and I can barely budge Oglethorpe. Employing a series of grunts and tugs and whatever leverage is available, we manage to get him to the edge of the trunk, where we pull so hard he crashes to the ground. It's frosty cold outside, and I think how hard the ground must be, and seriously doubt Richie and I will have the strength to dig a proper grave if we ever get the body where it's supposed to go.

Rudy surprises me by cutting an opening at one end of the bag and exposing Oglethorpe's feet. He shows his experience, saying, "There's rope in the trunk. Tie his ankles together and drag him."

We tie his feet together and I ask, "Where to?"

"You lead, I'll walk behind you."

"How will we know where to go?"

He aims the flashlight toward a small break in the bushes. "Follow the bouncing ball."

Richie and I begin the task of pulling Mr. Oglethorpe through the bushes. This turns out to be much easier than I anticipated, and within minutes Rudy says, "Okay, that's far enough."

24.

I CAN SEE from the light Rudy's flashlight gives off that we've entered a small clearing. Rudy is moving around in it, looking for something. Suddenly a wide beam of light flashes, and I realize he's turned on an electric lantern. There are three others next to it. He turns them on, and carries them far enough to illuminate a twenty foot square that includes a large tree. Next to the tree is a mound of dirt with two shovels propped against it, and next to that is a deep hole, the size of a grave.

"Okay guys," Rudy says. "It's show time."

We see his flashlight on our faces and realize he's aiming a video camera at us. I shout, "We're doing this against our will!"

Rudy laughs and says, "Yell all you want. There's no sound, dipshit. Now remove the plastic and let me get a close up of his face."

We do as we're told, and yes, it's definitely Oglethorpe.

"All right, now drag him to the edge of the grave, then take the rope off his feet and give it to me."

We do what he says. Then he nods at the hole in the ground. "Dump him in and fill it with dirt."

Even though the hard work has been done for us, it takes longer than I'd have thought to fill a six-foot grave with dirt. By the time we're finished, we're huffing so hard we can barely catch our breath. We look up and see the video camera still recording, only now it's on a tripod. Rudy can't hold it because he's got two sets of handcuffs in one hand and a gun in the other. And he's pointing the gun at us.

"That's good enough," he says. "Now put the shovels down and come over here."

Richie and I exchange a glance, then do as we're told. Rudy says, "Lie face down. Put your hands behind your backs."

When we're in position, he handcuffs us and tells us to stand.

Richie and I are not athletic. He might be less athletic than me, but it's a moot point because neither of us can get to our feet. Here we are, rolling, grunting and flopping around, making no headway at all.

"Can you believe this shit?" Rudy says.

"Where did you *find* these guys?"

Richie and I freeze where we are, startled to hear a second voice. Suddenly someone hoists Richie to his feet and there are more lights being placed around the tree. I angle myself to where I can see a young man and woman standing to the left of the tree with another gangster. The woman is sobbing quietly. Rudy is standing to the right of the tree, and there's a goon behind Richie, the one that pulled him to his feet. My eyes go back to Rudy, remembering the rope we tossed him a few minutes earlier. He's made a hangman's noose from it and looped it over the lowslung branch of the tree.

Richie is visibly shaken. Not by the noose, but by the couple standing before him. He screams, "What are you *doing*? This was never discussed! This was never part of the deal!" The goon behind him stuffs a ball in Richie's mouth and wraps tape around his head to hold it in place. Richie is still screaming, but his words are muffled and garbled. The gangster pushes Richie several feet forward, directly in front of the couple. The goon standing with the couple says, "This is him."

Richie screams something and shakes his head from side to side as if shouting "No!" His eyes are wide with terror.

The young man's face is twisted with rage. He says, "Are you absolutely certain?"

"One hundred percent."

The young man looks at me and says, "Who's he?"

Rudy says, "He's not involved. But this one, Richie, he's your guy."

The young man stares at Richie. "Do you have proof?"

Rudy walks over to the couple and hands them an envelope. "I found these in his desk drawer."

Richie screams and shakes his head again.

The young man and woman open the envelope and look at the photographs. I have no idea what they're seeing, but as the photos fall to the ground, the man lunges at Richie, who lets out a yelp and tries to run away. But Goon Number Two, the one behind Richie, grabs him and holds him while the young man punches his face again and again. I have no idea what's going on, and I'm still on the ground, but I try to work my way over to them. Goon Number One, standing next to the woman, points a gun at me and tells me to stay put.

When Richie's body goes slack, the young man finally stops hitting him. Then he falls to his knees and sobs. The woman puts her hand on his shoulder. Ten second later, Richie starts coming to. The young woman walks up to him, slaps him hard, and spits in his face. Then Goon Two walks Richie over to the noose and slips it around his neck. Richie's face is so full of blood it's hard to make out his facial features. Rudy tightens the rope to the point that Richie is standing on tiptoes to keep from being strangled. At this moment, God help me, an old joke goes through my depraved mind, and I hear my internal voice ask if maybe one of Richie's wishes was to be well hung.

I hate myself for having made that connection, but it's weird how the mind works when subjected to horrific violence. My friend is crying out in fear. Goon One leads the couple over to the tree. As Rudy keeps the rope taut, Goon Two pulls Richie's pants and underwear down to his ankles. He hands the young man a scalpel and says, "You still want to cut off his dick, now's a good time."

Richie screams and kicks the air with his right leg, trying to keep them away. He's sobbing and yelling and the scene is so terrifying I start to wretch.

The young man looks at the scalpel a long time, and finally says, "No."

Goon Two looks at the young woman and says, "How about you?"

She shakes her head.

Rudy says, "You still want us to hang him, though, right?"

The young couple look at each other. She says, "It won't bring Tracy back, but...yes. It will keep him from hurting some other child."

The man says, "Just do it quickly. We don't want him to suffer unduly. We just want justice for Tracy."

Rudy says, "We can hang him now, or after you leave. Depends on if you want to watch. One thing I'll say, it's not a pretty thing, watching a man hang. On the one hand, it might make you feel better. On the other, it might make you feel worse. He'll be dead in five minutes either way. But it's your wish. You make the call."

They speak to each other softly, and then embrace. The young man says, "We'll watch from a distance as long as we can. Then, if someone will walk us back to the car, we'd be grateful."

Rudy nods to the two goons, and they pick up lanterns and escort the couple to the edge of the clearing. As Richie and I scream, Rudy pulls the rope and Richie's feet come off the ground. He manages one blood-curdling scream but the noose chokes off any additional sounds. Richie is still alive and kicking the air. His eyes bug out and his face looks ghoulish. When he shits himself, the young man and woman can't take any more. They turn their backs to him, and the goons escort them away.

Rudy immediately releases the rope, and Richie falls to the ground. Rudy removes the rope from Richie's neck, and I start rolling across the ground toward them.

25.

WE'RE BACK IN my car, heading home. Having soiled his own clothes, Richie's wearing the extra underwear and pants I brought. He's looking out the window again, crying softly.

"Did you do it?" I said.

I slap the back of his head. "Answer me, you son of a bitch!"

I think about the obscene comment and gesture he made about Lissie last Sunday, when all this wish business started. What he'd said, and the way he said it while grabbing his crotch, had pissed Mike off.

Mike.

For a split second I wonder what's become of our friend. He was the first to fill out the list. I can only hope he's okay. But I can't concentrate on Mike right now. The idea of Richie being a child molester is too repulsive to allow me to focus on anything else.

"Tell me the truth, Richie. Did you do something to their little girl? I've known you twenty years."

"Relax, pipsqueak," Rudy says from the back seat. "He's never been within ten miles of their little girl."

"What? Then why—"

"Sally and Tom made a wish that their daughter's killer would be caught and hung from a tree. Of course, Tom wanted to cut his dick off, as well."

"I don't understand."

"We took the wish and found the guy, but too late. He'd already killed himself, hours earlier. Richie owed us a payment, so we decided to let him step in for the guy."

"He could've been killed!"

"He could've been run over by a bus while crossing the street this morning."

"That's not the point."

"Why, you think I can't get a bus?"

I blink my eyes in horror. "You're playing with people's lives!"

"I wouldn't call it playing."

"What if that guy had cut off Richie's dick?"

"Tell you the truth, I thought he would."

"What the fuck is *wrong* with you?"

"I were you, I'd dial it down. You don't hear Richie bitching about it."

He's right, I don't hear Richie bitching about it, and wonder why. In fact, now that I think about it, I don't recall Richie making a sound until the other goons showed up with Sally and Tom.

"Richie," I say. "What's going on here?"

"He's not much of a talker these days," Rudy says.

"What have you done to him?"

"We gave him three tasks."

"But you nearly killed him tonight. Hasn't he done enough?"

"Normally he'd be done by now. But he refused to honor the second one."

I drive in silence a few minutes. Then I ask, "What did he refuse to do?"

Rudy pauses a moment. "Normally I wouldn't say. But

now I'm thinking it might be a teaching opportunity. This gets a little tricky, so pay attention. Like I said, we got a wish list from Tom and Sally, to find the man who killed their daughter. The killer was Robby Billups. But we also got a wish list from Robby's mother, Margot."

"This is insane!"

"It's not such a big coincidence. Margot's first wish was that Robby would get professional help. Her second was that Tracy's parents would die."

"Why would you grant a wish like that?"

"Look at it this way: when we get a wish from someone to kill a grieving couple like Sally and Tom, we figure there has to be a connection to their little girl, Tracy."

"Which is how you found Robby in the first place."

"That's right. And a couple of days ago your friend, Richie, got the call."

"What call?"

"To kill Sally and Tom."

"What?"

"But he refused. So tonight we wanted to show him what happens when you refuse to pay back a wish."

What bothers me about what I'm learning is that there's a sort of logical pattern to the whole wish-granting and payback system. But some things aren't as easy to follow. "You told Richie to kill Tom and Sally before telling them about Tracy."

"Robbie Billups was dead, so we couldn't grant Tom and Sally's wish. So we decided to kill them, so Margot could get her wish. We gave the call to Richie. When he refused, we thought, why not grant both wishes? We'll tell Tom and Sally that Richie killed Tracy. By cutting off his dick and hanging him, they'd get two of their wishes. When we kill Tom and Sally, Margot gets one of *her* wishes."

My brain was fighting to keep up. I should have been horrified, but I was determined to comprehend the logic. I said, "And if Richie had died tonight?"

"You'd have gotten the call to kill Tom and Sally."

From my vantage point I could only see Richie's side and back. But I'd seen enough tonight to know he'd never be the same. "You'll let Richie go now, right?"

"He'll get the opportunity to kill Sally and Tom again, if that's what you mean."

"And after that, he still owes a fourth payment?"

"That's right. If he lives to do it, he'll be part of a group repayment."

"What does that mean?"

"When a number of people wish for the same thing, we lump them together, if possible. If twenty people want front row seats to a concert tonight, we'd fulfill twenty wishes in one shot."

"But that would be a group wish, not a repayment."

"True. Group repayments aren't as much fun as attending a concert."

"Tonight I've completed my first repayment," I say.

"Actually, you've made two. You just don't know it yet."

"What's the other one?"

"We'll let you know when the time is right."

"You made a video of us burying Oglethorpe. Why?"

"My boss likes to watch."

"Who's your boss?"

"Not your concern. But the video will also help prevent you from going to the cops."

"I could tell them you forced me."

"We've got the murder weapon, and your prints are all over it."

"That's not possible."

"We transferred them. Also, we've got a pair of your sneakers with Oglethorpe's blood on them. We've got...trust me, we've got plenty of evidence to put you away for life. But that's just a contingency. We've got something much better."

"What are you talking about?"

"We know your biggest weakness."

"I'm not following you."

"Let me put it this way: what's the most important thing in the world to you?"

Lissie!

He sees my expression.

"That's right, Buddy. We can do whatever we want to your precious Lissie. Anytime we want. And don't forget it."

26.

RUDY TELLS ME to take I-265 west to 64, and says I'll be dropping him and Richie off in Simpsonville.

"What's in Simpsonville?"

"You have to ask?"

"No."

"Say it."

"It's where Sally and Tom live."

"See? I keep telling our people you're not as dumb as you look. By the way, we've got a tracking device on your car. If you try to stop somewhere on the way home, we'll know it."

I know these people are well-funded, but I'm pretty sure he's bluffing. They couldn't possibly have someone watching me full time on a monitor.

Rudy says, "I can tell you don't believe me, so I'm gonna give you an example. When you get to the next exit, get off and try to hide somewhere."

I take the next exit and drive two blocks and park my car behind a strip center. In less than a minute a car pulls in front of me and the driver flashes his hibeam in my face. He gets out and walks to my window with his gun aimed at my face. He motions for me to roll down the window.

"You're not allowed to stop on the way home," he says. "You're not allowed to use a phone, or enter a business, or any other structure. Not even a porta potty."

He looks at Richie a long moment, then at Rudy. "Everything all right here?"

"I just wanted him to understand the rules."

The guy nods and walks back to his car and waits for me to pull out. I do, and get back on the interstate, headed for Simpsonville. I don't see him again, but I know he's back there in the distance.

I drop them off and watch Rudy lead Richie to a black sedan. Richie never said a word to me before getting out of the car, and even now there's not so much as a wave. I think back to the three guys who were hanging out in the basement of my split-level ranch less than a week ago, smoking a joint, dreaming about having sex with movie stars. As I watch Richie climb into the back seat I fear I will never see him again.

I check the clock on the dashboard and see I've been gone five hours.

All the way home, I'm trying to figure out how to make a phone call to the one person who might be able to help me, a contract killer named Donovan Creed. I just don't know how to make the call without getting caught.

I drive back to my place and put the car in the garage. I go inside and race up the stairs to our bedroom to check on Lissie, and find her sleeping on her side, just the way I left her. I look for her cell phone, find it, and try to place a call. But there's no dial tone. I pick up my home phone and hear a click. Rudy wasn't lying, they've tapped our phone.

I go back down the steps, out to the garage, and check the places where I hid random bricks of cash. They're all there. I go back inside the house, pour myself a shot of whiskey, down it in one gulp, head back up the stairs, and climb into bed with Lissie.

27.

"JESUS, BUDDY, HOW much did we drink last night?"

I wake up, startled.

"What?"

"I'm so groggy. Are you?"

According to the clock on the end table, it's nearly eleven. "Yeah, I feel like I'm in a fog. We were pretty lit."

"My God, I feel like I've been hit by a truck."

"I should have made you stop."

She sat up, tried to focus. "Oh, shit."

"What's the matter?"

"I'm still wearing my nightie."

"So?"

"We didn't make love."

"Oh. You're right. We must have passed out."

She smiles and kisses me on the cheek. "Well, we're not used to so much excitement. But Buddy?"

"Yeah?"

"Congratulations, superstar. I'm really proud of you."

"Thanks, hon."

Lissie gets out of the bed and stumbles slightly on her way to the bathroom, reminding me of Jinny, and how she stumbled when heading to the closet to fetch my money. *God, was that just yesterday?*

"Oh, God," Lissie moans from inside the bathroom. "Sorry,

but I'm going to be in here awhile."

"Okay, I understand."

"I feel like a beanbag that's been tossed one time too many."

I hear her retch, and then throw up. I run to the door. "You okay, baby?"

"Not feeling so good. I must have been *plastered* last night. I hope I didn't embarrass you."

"No, you were great. You remember dinner, right? And the concert?"

"Oh, my God, yes! And Perkins! I remember him walking me to the door."

"Right."

She vomits again. "God, I'm sorry, Buddy. I hate for you to see me like this."

I feel guilty as hell about the sedative and ask, "Is there anything I can do to help?"

"No. Please, just go downstairs or somewhere you can't hear me. I really don't want to gross you out."

"Okay, honey. I hope you feel better soon."

I feel like a complete shit heel. I'm happy about the million dollars in the garage, but I keep remembering Pete Rossman in the jet yesterday, telling me what was in the fine print of the Wish List Agreement:

"Your life."

I rush downstairs to the kitchen and fire up my computer, get online, and type in www.wishlist.bz. When the website loads, I look for the Agreement.

I find the little box that lets you read the fine print, and click it. I scroll up, down, reading the words, searching for loopholes. Specifically, I wonder if I can make new wishes to cancel out the old ones. But I'm no attorney. I can't make sense of all the legalese in the agreement. I start a new list and type the words *Never Harm Lissie*, and a message comes on the screen:

BUDDY, YOUR FOUR WISHES HAVE BEEN GRANTED.

IF YOU'D LIKE TO CREATE FOUR WISHES FOR LISSIE, PLEASE CONTINUE. IF NOT, DELETE THIS WISH, AND LEAVE THE SITE IMMEDIATELY.

Holy shit! I erase the wish and back myself off the website. I don't want Lissie involved with these bastards any more than she already is. Nor do I want more wishes that have to be repaid! I just want to be left alone with my wife and our life and our million dollars. I don't want to get arrested for killing my boss, and I don't want to be linked in the killing of Sally and Tom, and I don't want to know what made Jinny Kidwell agree to have sex with me. I wonder what the chances are that Rudy and the company will let me do my paybacks and leave us alone. It makes sense they would. If I participate, and do everything they ask, they should be willing to let me walk away.

Then I think about Richie and wonder what I'll do if they ask me to kill someone.

At that precise moment, there's a knock at the kitchen door. I jump up and look through the peephole.

And see Rudy.

28.

"WHAT ARE YOU *doing* here? Lissie's home!"

Rudy and I are on the porch. I've got the door closed, hoping Lissie doesn't come downstairs before I can get rid of him.

"How's she feeling this morning?" he says.

"You know about the sedative?"

"I know about everything."

"Then you should know she's a bit under the weather."

"No need to bite my head off, Champ, I was just trying to make conversation."

"Look, I just want out."

"Out of what?"

"This whole thing. The Wish List. I want out."

"I feel your pain."

"No, seriously, Rudy. What can I do to get my life back?"

"Give us two paybacks."

Hearing him say that reminds me of last night.

"What happened to Richie?"

"You'll be pleased to know he came through with flying colors."

"You're kidding."

"Amazing what you can do when your life depends on it."

"Will you really let us go if we do what you ask?"

"Why wouldn't we? You can't have an agreement unless

both parties fulfill their promises."

He's right! For the first time since meeting the guy, I'm beginning to get a glimmer of hope that everything that's happened can somehow be swept under the rug. Because what he just said is a hundred percent true: if both parties signed an agreement, and we both agreed to fulfill four requests, doing so should terminate the relationship. I've received four wishes, paid back two. It's a simple math equation.

Then he says, "You ever been in a fight?"

"What?"

"A fist fight."

"You mean, for real? A real fight?"

"Yeah."

"No, of course not. I don't know a thing about fighting."

"Yeah, that's what I figured."

"Why do you ask?"

"I signed you up to fight a guy tonight."

"You *what*?"

"Tonight at eight. We'll pick you up at seven."

"You can't be serious!"

"You know how you were asking me about the group payback last night?"

"What about it?"

"This is a perfect example. A bunch of people wished to see a fight between two guys with no training or experience."

"That doesn't make sense. Who would waste a wish on seeing a crappy fight?"

"It's not gonna be a crappy fight. It's gonna be a hell of a fight! And my money's on you, Champ!"

"I'm totally out of shape. There's no way I can win a fight. I can barely climb the stairs in my own house."

"You just need a little confidence."

"It's not possible. I can't fight, and don't want to."

"There are three motivations working in your favor," Rudy says, "and I'll tell you two of them now."

I'm staring vacantly. I don't believe in fighting. I'm terrified of confrontation. I can't stand the sight of blood. I once signed a petition to ban boxing! Last night, watching Tom punch Richie's face, I almost threw up. Jesus, it just hit me: Tom and Sally are dead.

Because their daughter's killer's mother wished it.

Rudy says, "Pay attention, Champ. Motivation number one is you'll have your third payback out of the way."

"You never told me what the second one was."

"I'll tell you tonight. The second motivation is even stronger. I can't wait to tell you."

"Just say it, okay? Say it and get out of here, before Lissie sees us."

"Okay, okay! Don't get your panties in a bunch. I was just trying to build suspense. The second motivation is, this is a fight to the finish."

"What?"

"Ain't it great? I mean, two pansies are gonna fight until one of them is pronounced dead."

"No! You can't! Please don't make me do this. Wait—you actually *can't* force me!"

"Excuse me?"

"You said so yourself."

"What're you talking about?"

"Yesterday you said you don't make people do things they don't want to do. You give them two, sometimes three choices, like with Jinny."

"I said that?"

"You did. Look, give me another choice. What's my

alternative?"

He looks confused. "Well, if I said it, I guess I'm bound."

"Okay, then. So give me something else."

"I'll make a deal with you. When we pick you up tonight, I'll give you an alternative, if you still want one."

"I'll want one."

"We'll see. But in case you choose to fight, bring a pair of shorts and tennis shoes, unless you want to fight barefoot."

"Are you *listening* to me? I'm not gonna fight tonight!"

"I heard you, Champ. Jeez, I'm not deaf. I'm just saying, in case you change your mind, that's what you should bring to wear."

"I won't change my mind."

"See you at seven, Champ."

"Stop *calling* me that!"

29.

LISSIE IS STILL groggy from the sedative, but with each hour that passes, her condition improves. Perkins told me to put the whole capsule in her drink, but half that amount would have been more than enough.

I've got a good excuse for going out tonight. I tell her Perkins is coming to pick me up for a meeting with my new client.

"When am I going to meet this Thomas Jefferson?" she says. "Will he be in the car tonight?"

"No, Perkins is taking me to the airport to meet his private jet. I think I'm meeting the CEO, too. But we shouldn't be out too late."

"I'm not used to these late night meetings. Is this going to be a regular thing?"

"No. It's just getting acquainted stuff."

By four in the afternoon, Lissie has recovered enough to wonder why I'm acting so strangely. "I can't remember you ever being more attentive, and yet you're completely distracted. What gives?"

I'm attentive because if worse comes to worse I could get beat to death tonight, in which case I'll never see her again. I'm distracted for the same reason.

"I'm just worried about you," I say. "And nervous about my meeting tonight."

"You'll be great," she says.

Actually, distracted isn't the best word to describe how I'm feeling. What I am is scared shitless. It's clear to me that Rudy wants me to fight, so the choice he gives me will probably be something worse than killing someone (or being killed) in the boxing ring.

But what could be worse than that?

At seven o'clock Rudy and Perkins pick me up and take me to an abandoned warehouse a half mile behind the airport at Standiford Field. There are two huge luxury busses in the parking lot, and two bouncers guarding the front door.

"What's in there?" I ask Rudy.

"The cage."

"What cage?"

"The one you're fighting in."

The cold sensation floods my body again. I know I'm pale with fear. I try to speak, but my voice comes out in a whisper. I swallow and try again. "What about our deal?"

"We'll get you in the dressing room, get your hands wrapped, and then I'm going to show you a quick video of your opponent. After that, if you still don't want to fight, I'll give you an alternate choice."

"Okay."

30.

THE DRESSING ROOM is nothing more than a woman's bathroom with two stalls and an oversized powder room that includes two sinks, a large mirror, a fabric couch, and a small Formica table with two scuffed, wooden stools, one of which I'm sitting on. On the counter, next to a sink, is a small monitor. Standing over me, applying tape to my hands is Gus, a grizzled old guy with cauliflower ears and a hopelessly broken nose. Gus, I'm told, is my cut man.

While Gus wraps my hands, Rudy and one of the bouncers hook up a video camera to the TV monitor. They're watching something on the screen, but their broad backs are blocking my view. At one point the bouncer guy turns and looks at me and shakes his head, which I take as a bad sign.

"All right," Rudy says. "Now rewind it a bit. Okay, that's good. Hit the pause button. Okay, that'll work."

They both turn to face me, but they're still blocking the screen. When Gus says he's done with my hands, Rudy asks him to step outside for a few minutes. When he opens the door to leave I can hear people yelling and chanting.

"The natives are getting restless," Rudy says.

The door closes and Rudy tells the bouncer guy to cut the lights.

Before he starts rolling the tape, Rudy says, "You wanted me to tell you the second thing you've done to pay us back."

He gestures to the monitor. "It's this."

The next three minutes are the worst of my life.

Afterward, when the guy flips the lights back on, the face I see in the mirror staring back at me is tear-streaked and filled with grief. I jump to my feet and run to the toilet and puke. I fall to my knees, sobbing, and puke again. I roll around on the floor, crying, moaning like a wounded animal. Minutes pass while my mind works to comprehend what I saw on the screen. When I finally get to my feet, there are two things I know beyond a shadow of a doubt: first, my life, as I knew it, is over. Second, I'm going to kill my opponent in the cage tonight, or die trying.

Rudy enters the doorway and calls out to me. "You ready to fight?"

I come out of the stall and stumble into him. He backs up a few steps and we're in the powder room again. I'm blind with rage, but I want to take my fury to an even higher level. I motion to the TV monitor.

"Play it again," I say. "In slow motion."

Rudy smiles broadly. "Whatever you say, champ!"

He rewinds the tape, presses a button, and nods to the bouncer to cut the lights.

I'm standing three feet from the screen, bracing my hands on the countertop. As the tape starts, I hear a loud drumming sound and look around to find the source.

It's me.

I'm tapping my fingers on the countertop, uncontrollably.

Like Jinny's husband, Pete Rossman had done.

I turn my attention back to the screen...

31.

THE QUALITY OF the video is excellent. There's a time signature on the bottom right. It starts at 1:05 a.m. with a shot of me, Rudy and Richie getting in the car and driving away. There's a slight jerk where they spliced the tape, and now it's 1:09 am, and the same camera picks up a man entering the garage. He's dressed in black, wearing a black ski mask similar to the ones Rudy and Richie had on. He removes a set of keys from his pocket and unlocks the door to my home. The camera switches to a view from the upstairs hallway, where we see the man climbing up the stairs. He pauses at our bedroom door, knocks, then waits a few seconds, then slowly opens the door and enters.

Another camera picks up the action in the bedroom. At this point it hasn't dawned on me that someone has gone to the trouble to place all these cameras in my home and garage, and they've obviously been there long enough to be tested for lighting and angles. It also hasn't dawned on me yet that the garage cameras would have revealed all the places I hid the cash.

What I do understand with total clarity is that a man is in my bedroom, standing over Lissie's sleeping, helpless body. Though it's dark in the room, I can see him push her shoulder a couple of times to see if she moves. She doesn't. Then he walks over to the doorway and turns on the light switch.

With the lights on, and the time showing 1:12 a.m., a camera directly over the bed takes over and shows the man kissing Lissie's face. The ski mask proves to be a hindrance to his intimacy, so he removes it, along with the rest of his clothing. Then he kisses her passionately, and starts removing her nightie.

The tape jumps again and it's 1:16 a.m. The man is performing oral sex on my wife's comatose body. I feel a white hot boil in the pit of my stomach. My heart aches as I watch her rape take place. Lissie trusted me and I want to die. I gave her a sedative, rendered her helpless, only to be violated by this human pond scum, and there is no pit deep enough to hide my anguish. I'm vaguely aware of the moaning sound coming from my mouth. I can taste the tears and snot dripping into my mouth and I want to fucking die.

I've never felt so powerless, never loathed myself to this degree. I want it to stop. If only I could go back in time and somehow make it stop. But it won't stop. In fact, the brutalization of my wife's helpless body has only just begun.

The tape jumps again and it's 1:28 a.m. The maggot is doing my wife missionary style. Every now and then he turns and winks at the camera. He stops for a minute to arrange her body in the most degrading pose the perverted mind of a rapist could imagine. Then he brutally assaults her.

He finishes quickly, and lies down beside her, spent. But he's not finished. Oh no. In fact, he's just getting started.

The tape jumps again, and it's 2:25 a.m. He's doing my sacred Lissie doggie style, slapping her ass, pulling her hair, mugging for the camera. The tape jumps again, three more times over the next two hours, but I can't share the unspeakable details of what he does to my poor Lissie.

But I know who he is.

I recognized him the instant he removed his ski mask.

In a few minutes I'll be in a cage with him, and I will do everything in my power to kill him.

32.

AT FIRST, SEEING him in my bedroom in the dark with my wife, I thought it had to be Pete Rossman, and figured he was getting me back for sleeping with his wife.

But it wasn't Pete Rossman.

It was my best friend Mike.

Mike, the guy who started the whole Wish List disaster, the guy who filled out his choices first, and told me his dream date was Katrina Bowden, the receptionist from *30 Rock*.

"Mike's first wish was to fuck my wife," I say to Rudy.

"Yeah, I asked him about that."

I stop crying long enough to look at Rudy's face. "What did he say?"

Rudy shrugs. "Said you're a sap who doesn't appreciate what you've got."

I nod. "Anything else?"

"You sure you want to hear it?"

I feel my jaw tighten. I release it, but it tightens again. "Yeah, I want to hear it."

"He said he's wanted to fuck her for years."

I nod.

"He also said she's a helluva fuck."

I know Rudy's pushing my buttons. I want to say something to him, curse him, kill him. But I deserve all this and more. And anyway, there's nothing he can say to make me feel any worse than I already do.

Except for this:

"Oh, Mike also wanted me to thank you for making it so easy. Said he loves the way you dressed her up, drugged her, and left her all alone, helpless, on your marital bed. And..."

I nod.

..."he said he can't wait to fuck her again."

I squeezed my eyes shut.

Rudy says, "I don't want to rush you, Champ, but that sound you hear outside means they're ready for you."

I look at him and realize there's something he hasn't told me yet, something he's saving.

"What haven't you told me about Mike?" I say.

"I'll tell you when you get in the cage, just before the bell sounds."

33.

I'M IN AN iron cage, glaring at Mike. He's meeting my stare, and has a strangely determined look on his face. We're surrounded by forty men in various stages of inebriation. The cage is small, maybe twelve feet by twelve, and is completely enclosed. There are no announcements, no introductions. The referee tells the crowd what to expect:

"Each round is three minutes, with a oneminute break. There will be as many rounds as needed until one man is pronounced dead. Can I have the corner men, please?"

The two bouncers enter the cage and stand at opposite ends. They are barefoot and barechested, wearing only shorts, and looking very mixed martial artsy. The referee continues:

"If at any time the action stops for fifteen seconds, the corner men will get involved. And you know what that means!"

I have no idea what it means, but the "crowd" obviously knows, because they're cheering wildly.

As the referee directs us to our corners, I see Rudy standing just outside the cage behind my stool. The crowd noise is growing.

"Here's the thing," Rudy says.

"Yeah?"

"Mike's fourth wish."

"What about it?"

"We haven't granted it yet. He has to kill you to get it."

The crowd noise is almost deafening. They smell blood and want the carnage to start.

"Tell me!"

Rudy looks at me in a way I could never forget, and yells, "We didn't let him do what he wanted."

"What are you saying?"

As the bell sounds to begin the first round I hear Rudy shouting above the crowd noise.

"He wants to chain her to his basement wall for the rest of her life!"

I turn to look at Rudy and feel a fist crash into the back of my skull.

The blow sends me reeling, and I'm knocked stiff-legged into the side of the cage. Mike jumps on my back and starts raining blows on the top of my head. Between his weight, my being off balance, and his furious attack, I go down. Had Mike ridden me to the floor it might have been over before I landed the first punch. But Mike's left leg gets hooked under my hip, and when I hit the canvas, his leg takes the brunt of my weight. When I roll over, he grabs his knee in agony. I quickly jump on him and start flailing away until I can barely breathe. Mike's arms were pinned under my knees throughout the assault, which means I landed at least forty clean shots to his face and head. But when I stop swinging to inspect the damage, I'm shocked to see I haven't even drawn blood.

I can't believe I'm this exhausted. Meanwhile, Mike is reenergized. He flips me off him and gets to his feet. He's favoring his left leg, but it's not keeping him from coming after me. Just as I'm about to stand, he tackles me and bites the back of my upper thigh. I let out a yelp and try to get away, but he's got his legs wrapped around mine and I can't get out from under him. He continues to bite my leg and I'm almost delirious with pain, but before he can do any more damage, the bell rings to end round number one.

One of the bouncers pulls Mike off me and pushes him to his stool. The other one drags me to mine, and Gus starts working on my thigh wound.

"Don't worry," he says, "I'm a great cut man."

"Good thing."

"Never had to work on an ass cut before, though."

From behind me I hear Rudy say, "You guys fight like old people fuck."

I have no idea what that means, but his next comment makes a lot of sense: "It takes time to beat a man to death. Save your energy. Make every shot count."

I wonder if he has any specific advice. He does: "Kick his bum knee."

For the next three rounds I let Mike use up his energy trying to rush in and paste me with his fists. Most of the time his punches miss me, and when they connect, they don't have much power. I don't land a single punch in rounds two, three and four, but I do manage to kick his knee several times in each round.

Now we're in the fifth round and he sees it coming, and when I fake the kick, he moves away, but straight back, and I'm able to land a blow to his cheek, just hard enough to make him stumble on his bad leg, exposing his right knee, which I kick with all my might. When he goes down I don't bother trying to hurt him with my fists like I did in the first round. I've come to realize that neither of us has any real punching power. But my kicks are working, so I start kicking him while he's down. He tries to catch my foot with his hands, but I'm keeping my kicks low and fast, and they're not doing much damage, but they're doing some, and just as the bell rings, I manage to kick his wrist and when he screams, I get the feeling things are going my way.

In round six we're both so weary the action lags and the referee calls time out and announces we're involving the corner men. He explains what that means:

"For the balance of the round, each fighter gets a free punch. After both fighters land ten punches, the round ends. Red corner goes first."

Our bouncers bring us to the center of the ring. Mine pins my arms behind me and holds me as Mike lands a solid punch. I catch the full force of the blow on my upper cheek, just below my left eye, and this one causes serious damage. I go all wobbly and nearly fall down. My eyes are glazed, and when I look down at the canvas, I see spots of blood dripping on it. I focus on Mike's face. He's sneering at me. He knows he's stronger than I am, and knows I can't win this type of fight.

He's right. My punches have virtually no power. I can't even make him bleed.

But I have an idea.

As his corner man pins his arms, I wind up with my right hand. But instead of launching it, I kick his right knee with every ounce of strength I've got. He howls with pain and shifts his weight to his left leg, which proves to be too much, and, but for his corner man holding him up, Mike would have crashed to the canvas.

The damage I inflicted with that perfect kick is evident. Mike can barely stand up, and his next punch comes in at less than half power. On my turn I kick him again. He makes a pathetic attempt to kick me on his next turn, but he loses his balance and his foot barely grazes me.

My turn.

I fake the kick and Mike is so worried about it landing, he tries to jump out of the way. But his corner man holds him steady, and Mike's face drops into perfect position and I strike his nose with all my might. And this time I draw blood.

When Mike's bouncer releases his arms, Mike touches his nose. He's got tears in his eyes and when he realizes his nose is broken, most of the fight in him has gone. He winds up and launches a roundhouse punch that takes so long to reach me, I'm able to duck my head, which means his punch lands on my skull. He screams in pain and I think his right hand might be broken. I try to land my final punch on his broken nose, but he gets it out of the way. I do manage to hit his eye flush, and figure that's going to start swelling up before long.

In the corner, Gus finally has the opportunity to work on my eye. The referee announces the next round will be fought the normal way unless the action stops for fifteen seconds. I hear Rudy urging me to keep kicking Mike's knees.

But I have a better idea.

Since I can't punch hard enough to hurt him, and since my legs are in good shape and Mike's are not, I decide to rush him. Not like he rushed me earlier, when trying to get in close enough to hit me, but to rush him and push him down. Mike attempts to land a big right hand, but I jump back in time to avoid it, and push him squarely in the chest with both hands. His bad knees give way and he falls to the floor. With his face an open target, I kick it until he brings his hands up to protect it, which leaves his ribs unprotected. I kick them until he brings his hands down, and then I kick his face again. Mike's in bad shape and getting worse. I get myself in a zone and keep kicking him wherever I find an opening. I'm thinking about how Mike is fighting to win my wife, while I'm fighting to keep her. He's got everything to gain, and I've got everything to lose. But while I cheated on Lissie, he raped her. And, like Perkins said, Lissie deserves better.

34.

I'M LYING ON the couch in the ladies'room, while Gus patches me up. My ears are ringing and I've got double vision. Every part of my body is aching and sore, and I realize I've taken a much harder beating than I thought.

"Where's Rudy?" I say.

"Collecting his money, I think."

It's just me and Gus in the dressing room.

"Thanks for your help," I say.

"My pleasure."

"Can I ask a favor?"

"You can ask. Don't mean I'll grant it."

"Can I borrow your cell phone?"

He thinks about it. "Twenty bucks."

"In my bag," I say.

He hands me his cell phone and crosses the room to get my bag. I dial the number my sister made me memorize a year ago, and silently pray it's still in service.

It rings several times, and finally he answers, saying, "Creed."

"Mr. Creed, this is Buddy Pancake. I'm in trouble."

I hear Creed say to someone, "Wait. You lost an earring." Then I hear a woman scream. Then Creed says, "Buddy, you're a pain in the ass."

"Sorry, Mr. Creed."

He pauses a moment, then says, "What kind of trouble have you gotten yourself into this time, Buddy?"

"The worst kind."

He sighs. "Where are you?"

PART TWO

DONOVAN CREED

1.

BUDDY PANCAKE WAS in Louisville, Kentucky, in an abandoned warehouse behind Standiford Airport, claiming he'd just beaten a man to death in a boxing match.

I said, "Get real."

He said, "No, I'm serious."

"No offense, Buddy," I said, "but my jock strap could kick your ass."

"Swear to God, Mr. Creed. They're forcing me to kill people."

"Who is?"

"There's a website, wishlist.bz. They grant wishes."

"To dying children?"

"No, not like that. You get four wishes, anything you want. But then they start making you pay them back by digging graves and killing people."

I frowned. "Buddy, your bullshit call ruined my perfect evening."

Buddy lowered his voice to a whisper. "I can pay you a half million dollars to protect Lissie."

"Who's Lissie?"

"My wife."

I didn't need the money, but half a million dollars was a staggering amount to a guy like Buddy Pancake.

"I forgot where you work," I said.

To someone on his end, Buddy said, "You can have all the money in my bag if you'll give me two minutes alone." There was a short pause, and then to me he said, "I'm a loan officer at Midwest Commercial Savings and Loan, here in town."

"You embezzled how much altogether?"

"It's not like that. The Wish List people gave me the money."

"That was one of your wishes?"

"Yes, sir."

"Bullshit."

"No, I swear."

"Buddy, I'm not in the mood."

"What do you mean?"

"No one wishes for a half million dollars. You probably asked for a million."

He paused before saying, "I was hoping to keep some of it."

"Who are we dealing with?"

"You mean in the company? The Wish List people?"

"Yeah."

"I only know a guy named Rudy, and a limo driver named Perkins. But this is an extremely powerful group of people, Mr. Creed."

"Yeah, Perkins the limo driver sounds terrifying."

"I'm serious, God damn it!"

He couldn't be. "Give me a for instance, besides the money."

"One of my wishes was to have sex with Jinny Kidwell."

"The actress?"

"Yes, sir."

"And did you?"

"Yes, sir."

"No shit?"

"I swear. But then they made me kill this bastard exfriend

of mine in a fight tonight. He raped my wife and I killed him. They say I still owe them another payment for the wishes they granted. And they threatened my wife. You're the only one I can turn to. You've got to help me."

"Are you willing to part with the full million?"

He sighed. "If that's what it takes."

"Is your life in danger?"

"I'm pretty sure it is."

"You had sex with Jinny Kidwell."

"Yes, sir."

"Where can we meet?"

"They've got cameras in my house, wiretaps on my phones."

"The phone you're using is tapped?"

"No. I'm using a stranger's phone. But they'll be back any minute."

"I'll be at your place by six a.m."

"Let me give you my address."

"Save your breath. I've got people. What were your other wishes?"

"They're coming. I gotta go."

2.

I TRY NOT to judge people. I really do try.

But if you're recruiting a loser army, Buddy Pancake is the first guy you want. Still, I'm willing to protect him and his wife for two reasons:

The first is Buddy's sister, Lauren.

Lauren Jeter had been a close friend for many years. She was an extraordinary hooker, whose client list included half of Cincinnati's movers and shakers. When Governor Eliot Spitzer's prostitution scandal broke in New York, certain Cincinnati lawmakers worried for their reputations. A few went so far as to threaten Lauren to keep her mouth shut in the event local news reporters decided to investigate the prostitution situation in Cincinnati. Concerned for her safety, Lauren told Buddy if anything ever happened to her, he should contact me.

Something did happen.

She got murdered.

Knowing the Cincinnati cops wouldn't dig too deeply into her case, I took it upon myself to track down her killer. It took me less than two days to find him: not a paranoid politician, as I'd suspected, but a sniveling real estate salesman with anger issues. I devoted two full days to the task of making him pay for what he'd done.

For the bulk of my life, my closest female friends have been hookers and killers, and if you want to judge me by that, go for it.

But don't judge them.

And especially don't judge Lauren Jeter.

Lauren had been a terrific provider. She was always happy to see me, always made me feel wanted. She was a gifted listener, an excellent therapist who tried her best to understand me. At one point, Lauren endured a great deal of pain on my behalf, in order to help me convince my exwife to break off her engagement to a guy who was all wrong for her. Like the finest women who've touched my life, Lauren was so much more than a caring companion, great conversationalist, or good lay. She excelled at not judging me, and making our time together memorable. She was one of the highlights of my life, and I miss her terribly.

All that's left of her is her kid brother, Buddy Pancake.

Doesn't hardly seem fair, does it?

The second reason I'm willing to help Buddy: my girlfriend, Rachel Case, lives in Louisville, and I haven't seen her in months. It would be nice to spend some time with her, and see how she's doing.

It was nine-thirty. I was in Chicago, with access to a number of private jets that could get me to Louisville in under an hour, so I had a world of time before our six a.m. meeting.

I fired up my laptop and typed wishlist.bz in the address bar. Once on the website, I read the promos and comments but decided not to make any wishes. Instead, I called my old friend, Lou Kelly. When he answered I said, "Where's Jinny Kidwell?"

"The actress?"

"Uh huh."

"You want to hold or have me call you back?"

"Call me back. I've got to pack."

"Gimme ten minutes."

Twenty years ago, Lou and I worked as hired assassins for the CIA in Europe. I was early twenties, Lou was forty. We survived that gig for twelve years and eventually made our way stateside, where I landed a job killing terrorists for Homeland Security. Lou headed up my intelligence team. At the height of the action, I had a dozen assassins on my team, helping me keep democracy safe. During my down time I performed freelance hits for the mob.

Six months ago I managed to steal billions of dollars from some of the world's most lethal people. After banking the big score, I retired from the government and mob killing jobs. I'd been told that once in, you can never get out alive, but I had a plan. First, I told both organizations I would consider future requests for work. Second, I set up five hundred million dollar annuities for Darwin, my Homeland Security boss, and Sal Bonadello, crime boss for the Midwestern United States. The money would be paid to their numbered accounts monthly by my lawyers, a million dollars a month for the rest of their lives, and their kids' lives, with one stipulation: all future payments would cease upon my death.

My plan worked.

Darwin and Sal no longer want to kill me.

They want to *protect* me!

Lou Kelly was a trusted member of the team that helped me obtain the huge score, and because of all our years together, his share of the take was also five hundred million, all in cash. Unfortunately, during the heist, the size of the prize got to Lou, and he tried to kill me and take my share.

Despite our trust issues, Lou and I were able to rebuild a working relationship. I let him keep his half-billion dollars from the heist, along with his life, and in return he provides the intelligence and computer expertise I require from time to time.

Lou is the best in the business. He had the answer on Jinny before I finished packing, and that's fast, since I travel light.

"She's on location in Hannibal, Missouri."

"Which hotel?"

"No hotel. A Trailer. In Riverview Park."

"A trailer?"

"A movie star trailer. Trust me, it's nice."

"What type of security do they have?"

"I'll have to get back to you on that," he said, and we terminated the call.

I contacted one of the many charter flight companies in Chicago I knew, and selected a Lear 45 for the short flight. As I boarded and waited for the engines to fire, Lou called to describe what the satellite photos had revealed about the security team guarding the actors'trailers in Riverview Park. Thirty minutes later I touched down at Hannibal Regional Airport.

Lou Kelly used to book my jets and drivers, but like I said, the trust ain't what it once was, so I've been forced to handle my own travel arrangements. Climbing down the jet's gangway, I was pleased to see my driver waiting beside a black sedan with all four doors open, as I'd specified.

"Can I trust you?" I said.

"Of course, sir."

"Your name?"

"Harrison Ford."

"Okay, Harrison. Please remove your jacket and place it on the hood of the car. Then assume the position while I pat you down."

"Sir, I can assure you—"

"I'm sure you can, and I've told you how. Now let's see you do it."

I noticed the pilots standing beside me appeared to be concerned. I shrugged at them as if to say, "What's with this guy, huh?" But that seemed to make them even more nervous, so I said, "Relax. I'm good with you guys."

The Lear captain said, "His name really Harrison Ford?"

"It's a code name. Still, you can't be too sure with a new driver."

I saw them give each other an uneasy look.

"Guys, I spent weeks checking you out. I know everything about you." I paused, looked them squarely in the eyes, and said, "Everything. I could demonstrate my knowledge of your lives, but you already seem nervous enough. Let's just say we're cool. I'm sure Harrison Ford will become a trusted friend tonight, as well. It's just that I haven't had time to check him out yet. Hannibal's a small town, and I don't have any contacts here."

My reassuring talk with the pilots didn't have the effect I intended, so I shrugged, patted my driver down, searched his car, and found nothing more sinister than a couple of tuna fish sandwiches and an unopened bottle of water. I had him climb in first, and I took the rear seat directly behind him, and we drove to Riverview Park, where I saw the movie set guards on duty.

"Keep driving," I said. He took me a quarter mile past the entrance, then I had him turn right on a road that ran parallel to the park. "Follow it to the end, and let me out. Meet me here when I call, which I'm guessing will be an hour or so."

He dropped me off and I jogged across the grass, toward the trailers that housed the movie stars. It was a short run, well under a mile, and when I came up behind Jinny Kidwell's trailer, I could see there were no guards stationed there, which confirmed Lou Kelly's suspicion that they were rental cops, not pros. I picked the lock and entered her trailer through the back door.

Once in, I realized I was alone. I knew Jinny was on site, so I decided to wait in her bedroom. While waiting, I took out a penlight, held it in my teeth, and searched through her belongings.

Forty minutes later I heard her come in the door. Lou had told me that Jinny's husband, Pete Rossman, was here from time to time, but I could tell from the sound of the footsteps out front that she was alone. She busied herself in the kitchen a few minutes before entering her bedroom.

I had my hand over her mouth before she'd gone three feet. She tried to scream, but my thumb was pressed so hard against her neck that all she could manage was a whisper.

"I'm not here to hurt you," I said, "I just want some information. Do you understand?"

She did her best to nod.

"That said, if you make a sound louder than a whisper, I'll kill you. Do you believe me?"

Again, she tried to nod.

"Good. I'd hate to harm you in any way, since I'm a huge fan. I'm only here to ask you about a company called Wish List, a guy who works with them named Rudy, and a guy with whom you recently had sex, named Buddy Pancake."

The light from the hallway illuminated her face. She appeared gaunt, and ill.

"Relax, Jinny. All I want is information, okay?"

Her green eyes were big as saucers, and full of fear. She mouthed the words, "Please. Don't hurt me."

I said. "Are you sick? I have a thing about germs."

She shook her head no.

"Anorexic?"

She shook her head again.

"I saw you last week on the Academy Awards. Nice dress."

She nodded.

"Guess the TV really does add ten pounds, huh?"

Her body was trembling. A couple of tears spilled from her eyes.

I said, "I'm going to remove my hand. For the record, I'm okay if you want to scream. But if you do, I'll have to kill the guards. I'm only asking you to whisper in order to protect them. Other than being inept, they haven't done anything wrong, and don't deserve to die. But it's your call."

I released my hold on her neck, and helped her sit on her bed.

"Can I switch on the light?" she said.

"I'd like that."

She turned the knob on her bedside lamp and looked at me. She rubbed her neck.

"Who are you?" she asked.

"Let's do it this way," I said. "Why did you have sex with Buddy Pancake?"

3.

JINNY KIDWELL GAVE me some bullshit story about paying back into the system that helped her become a star, but I wasn't buying. I covered her mouth again with my left hand, produced a switchblade in my right, and told her I was serious about getting some answers.

Jinny was a beautiful, pampered star, and I figured getting her to talk would be as easy as getting the President to do a photo op.

But I was wrong.

When I removed my hand from her mouth, she said, "It's okay if you want to kill me."

"I don't want to kill you. I just want to know why you fucked Buddy Pancake."

"You'll have to be content with the answer I gave you."

I frowned. This was new territory for me. Usually, I make a threat and people shit all over themselves. There could only be one explanation.

"You don't believe I'll kill you," I said.

"I do believe it."

"The answer you gave me about paying back into the system was a lie."

"Yes."

"But you're refusing to tell me the truth?"

"Yes. I'm refusing to."

"Why?"

"I—I can't say."

"Can't or won't?"

"Won't."

"Then I'll have to kill you." I moved the knife to the edge of her throat.

She started to cry. "Wait," she said.

I smiled.

But instead of telling me the truth, what she said was, "Before you kill me, can I call my husband and tell him I love him?"

4.

I DIDN'T KILL Jinny Kidwell at that time.

Instead, I looked into those endless eyes and said, "I'm obviously missing something. Something so important to you it's worth dying to cover up."

We sat on the bed a minute, looking at each other. Outside the trailer, maybe a mile down river, I heard a muffled whistle, as a barge prepared to navigate the next section of river.

"Maybe the best question isn't why you slept with Buddy Pancake," I said. "That was obviously a payback."

Jinny looked at her hands in her lap and said nothing.

"I should have asked about the wishes you made."

She said, "There were three silly ones, and the one I'm willing to die for."

"And this huge wish required the payment of sleeping with Buddy Pancake?"

"And giving him a million dollars in cash."

"What else have you had to do?"

"Tell my husband what I've done."

"And?"

"And I had to get him to make four wishes of his own on the website."

"And he did?"

She shrugged. "He loves me."

"So you have two more payments to make?"

"That's what they tell me."

"Rudy?"

"And the others."

"You know their names?"

"No."

"Scary guys?"

Her face took on a thoughtful expression. "Not as scary as you. No offense."

If Jinny wasn't afraid of what they might do to her, she must be afraid of what they might *not* do. Like grant her wish. I took a minute to ponder what Buddy had told me about the wishes and paybacks. "How many of your wishes have come true?"

"Three."

I nodded. "The little ones."

"So far."

"And you're waiting on the big one."

She nodded.

"And the big one is so important that if it doesn't come true, something will happen that is worse to you than dying tonight."

She didn't reply.

"You were willing to have sex with Buddy Pancake and give him a million dollars. What else would you be willing to do to get your wish?"

She squeezed her eyes shut, and two little puddles of tears raced each other down her cheeks.

I said, "Are you aware they made Buddy Pancake kill someone tonight with his bare hands?"

She gave me a sudden look of horror. Then her facial muscles went slack and she stared at her hands again. I watched her go through these emotions with great curiosity.

“You’re willing to sleep with a complete stranger, pay a million dollars, and even let people die in order to get this wish?”

She didn’t look up, didn’t speak, but her shoulders moved slightly, and I could tell she was crying softly.

“And just so we’re clear, you’re willing to let me kill you rather than tell me what you wished for.”

She finally looked up at me. Adding in the fact that Jinny Kidwell is damned good at what she does for a living, I could tell she wasn’t acting. She was in anguish, and her face ran the whole gamut of looks. She was frightened, horrified, humiliated, defeated...and somehow, hopeful.

“Must be one hell of a wish,” I said.

5.

"PLEASE, MR. CREED. I have a wife and kids at home."

It was 1:30 a.m.

At seventy-five miles per hour with no stops along the way, Hannibal to Louisville is a five hour drive. Harrison Ford was too jittery to handle the wheel, so I fastened him to the front passenger headrest with sealing tape to help him stay put. That was two hours earlier, and he hadn't stopped blubbering since.

"You're an annoying person," I said. "Anyone ever tell you that?"

"I'm sorry, I don't mean to be."

"I'd hoped you'd find this fun. I'd hoped you'd want to be my regular driver whenever I'm in the area. But you don't seem to have the temperament for it."

"I don't. I just want to go home."

"So you've said. A hundred times."

"Can you just give me a rough guess as to when that might happen? If you can tell me that, I'll feel a lot more comfortable."

I looked at him and shook my head. Our relationship wasn't working out. "Look, Harrison," I said. "You'll be back with your family tomorrow afternoon, Tuesday at the latest, dead or alive."

That made him even more nervous, so I added, "You have my word on that."

"Dead or alive?"

"Your choice. How you behave today makes a big difference."

"If I don't call my wife, she's going to be worried. If I don't come home, she might call the police."

"She's not expecting you before midnight. But don't worry, you can call her at the next stop."

"When will that be?"

"Couple hours."

"I'm going to need to pee before then."

"Feel free to do so. It's your car, after all."

"Look, Mr. Creed, you can't just—"

I knocked him unconscious with my fist. Something I should have done hours ago.

Two hours later we crossed the Crawford, Indiana county line into Harrison. I took the first exit and doubled back on the two lane to a gravel road I'd used a couple of times before that led to a dense, secluded area. After a few minutes I found the dirt road I was seeking, and followed it until it dead ended in the woods. I put the limo in park and kept the lights on.

Then I got out and walked to the back of the car and opened the cabin door and pulled Jinny Kidwell's lifeless body off the back seat.

6.

JINNY WAS UNCONSCIOUS, not dead, but by the time I got her wrist chained to a tree in the deep woods, she had begun to stir. I chained Harrison Ford to another tree, twenty feet away. I didn't know how long I'd be gone, and didn't want my prisoners to get dehydrated, so I took six bottles of water from the limo bar and divided them up, along with the blankets I'd brought from Jinny's trailer.

Then I forced Jinny and Harrison to scream at the top of their lungs, until their voices were raw, and waited to see if anyone showed up to help them. No one did. I drove away, waited twenty minutes, then returned, and found them sitting by their respective trees, crying. I think they'd probably gotten their hopes up when hearing the car approach, but were saddened to learn it was me.

I hung around a few minutes and listened patiently as they gave me all their reasons why I shouldn't leave them there, and then I left them there.

7.

BUDDY'S HOUSE WAS a baby shit yellow split-level ranch, with green shutters and clogged gutters. It was the second house on a wide, tree-lined street that featured a dozen similar homes. Buddy and Lissie's subdivision consisted of six through streets and four deadend cul de sacs, eighty-three homes in all. A nice middle class subdivision, from what I could tell by jogging it twice and studying everything within my field of vision. Specifically, I was looking for anything out of place: a limo other than mine, a van that might contain people with surveillance equipment, gangsters guarding the house, a mariachi band, a conga line filled with cartoon characters...

But nothing caught my eye except for the sad-faced octogenarian two blocks over, who walked to the center of his yard to retrieve his newspaper. He stood out because he was dressed in nothing more than an open bathrobe and a giant adult diaper.

"You think it's easy?" he yelled. "Huh? You think it's easy?"

I had no idea. But it looked pretty easy. As I passed him he yelled, "I get no visitors! You think it would kill them to show up once in a while? All I ask is one time, to have some visitors."

I made a mental note of his address.

Other than him, I saw nothing. Buddy was right. These Wish List people were good.

What I did expect to see was Buddy. On his porch, out by

his mailbox, looking out his window, or just standing in his driveway. After all, we had an appointment. Having offered me a million dollars to protect his wife, he'd have been here, if he had a choice.

I needed to establish contact. Unless I broke into his home, I wouldn't know if anyone was holding a gun on him and Lissie. And if someone did happen to be inside, guarding them, I could get killed trying to break in. Therefore, a phone call seemed in order.

Buddy had told me his phone was bugged, but I didn't intend to say anything that should raise any eyebrows. But when I called, Lissie answered frantically.

"Buddy?"

I disguised my voice. "Actually, I'm calling for Buddy. Is he there?"

She paused a few seconds, trying to place my voice. It probably seemed familiar to her. My friend and former associate, Callie Carpenter, claims my fake voice is terrible. She swears I sound like Sponge Bob Square Pants.

Lissie said, "Mr. Jefferson?"

I said, "No..."

"Perkins?"

"No, ma'am. I'm sorry. Is Buddy there?"

"Who is this?"

I hung up. Although nothing concrete had been said between us, I'd learned a few things: Buddy wasn't home. Lissie had been expecting his call. And she thought he was with a Mr. Jefferson, or Perkins, the limo driver Buddy had referred to as being dangerous.

I believed there were no gangsters in the house with Lissie because I, myself, have held people hostage in their homes, and when the phone rang, I always reminded them what to say and how to say it before answering. Since Lissie had answered my call on the first ring, I doubted there was any dangerous physical presence in her home at that time.

But I knew that would change quickly, because Rudy's people were not only monitoring the interior of the house with cameras, they were also monitoring Buddy's phone. They would immediately send a car to make a surveillance sweep of the neighborhood after hearing my call. I mean, who phones someone at the crack of dawn using a disguised voice, unless they're up to something? I didn't want to be out on the street when they arrived, but if I loitered too long near the house waiting to ambush them, some early rising neighbor might see me and call the cops.

I quickly broke into the side door of Buddy's garage, entered it, and looked around for hidden cameras. Within a minute I found three, along with two bundles of cash. Did I mention Buddy was a complete sap? I left the money where I found it, and kept searching the garage until I saw a can of black spray paint, which I squirted onto the pinhole cameras that had filmed my every move.

If I knew where the money was, the Wish List people certainly knew. So why would they let Buddy keep it? Was it possible they intended to abide by their agreement? If so, Buddy might be wrong about Lissie's life being in danger.

Unless he refused to repay one of his wishes.

I had originally intended to break into Buddy's house, render Lissie unconscious, and get her to safety. I mean, it would have been nice if I could have knocked on her door and said, "Lissie, I'm a former CIA assassin. Buddy hired me to protect you. Let's go!" Or maybe call her and tell her to run out the door and go somewhere safe. That would be simple, and she could probably get away before the Wish List people could get a car here. But I had no reason to think she'd listen to a total stranger. For one thing, she'd been hovering over the phone, waiting for Buddy to call. She wouldn't just run away without hearing from him. For another, they probably had a tracking device on her car, so she wouldn't get far. Nor was she likely to willingly climb into a car with me.

Since the cameras had caught me in the garage, I'd have to scrap my original plan. There simply wasn't enough time to get Lissie to my car before they arrived.

And there was something else.

While searching the garage I found something that changed the playing field and made me want to leave immediately: I'd seen wires running through one of the vents. The kind of wires demolition experts attach to plastic explosives.

8.

I BURST OUT the garage door, jumped the back fence, and ran to the far side of the subdivision, where I'd parked the limo. As I threw the car in gear, I wondered why they hadn't detonated the garage the moment I sprayed the camera lenses. But they hadn't, and that probably meant...well, I didn't know what that meant. But I booked it out of there and hoped Lissie would be safe until I came up with another plan. It would be difficult, since all the action would be taking place in a self-contained neighborhood, where at least one garage was wired with explosives. Also, I knew next to nothing about who I was dealing with, how many were involved, or what their motives were.

I thought again about calling Lissie, but decided against it. I knew Rudy's people were listening, and what if they decided it would be easier to just blow her up? If her garage was wired with explosives, who's to say her entire house wasn't set to blow?

And what about Buddy?

Hours ago, his last words to me were, "They're coming. I've got to go." So whoever "they" were, and I'm guessing Rudy and Perkins, maybe some others—they obviously took Buddy somewhere against his will. Since Lissie was still home, waiting for Buddy, she probably didn't know about Wish List, or where Buddy was.

They had to be using Lissie to force Buddy's cooperation. As in, "Do what we want, or something bad happens to Lissie."

I called my tech expert, Lou Kelly. When he answered, I said, "Is there any way to remotely remove a listening device from someone's land line?"

"Not that I'm aware of," he said.

"Then I've got a problem," I said. "A woman's life is in danger, her house is being watched, and her phones are tapped. I need to save her. Any suggestions?"

"Have you called the phone company to report a possible bug?"

"What good would that do?"

"If they came to the house, maybe you could borrow one of their uniforms and join them."

"Great idea!"

"Really?"

"No, it's a lousy idea. But it helped me think of a great idea."

"Tell me. No, wait. Why is it a lousy idea?"

"You know how long it takes the phone company to respond to problems? I'd be waiting all day."

"So what's the good idea?"

"I'll tell you later."

I pulled into a convenience store a couple of miles from Lissie's neighborhood, and parked by one of the gas pumps. After making sure no one was nearby, I retrieved one of the disposable cell phones from my kit and called 911. When the operator answered I disguised my voice with a Middle Eastern accent and told her I was calling in a bomb threat. I didn't want to give them Lissie's address because the Wish List guys might decide to blow her up if the cops showed up at her place. But I wanted to get as many police in the neighborhood as fast as possible, in order to discourage Rudy from paying a visit. So I gave them the address of Lissie's neighbor, the guy in the diaper who gets no visitors.

"Sir, we take bomb threat calls very seriously."

"That is precisely why I called you."

"You sound like a cartoon character."

"This may be, and yet I can assure you the bomb threat is real."

She sighed. "Your name, please?"

I could tell the call was going south, so I screamed, "Dogs! You will never stop us! Death to the infidels! Allah Akbar!"

Then I hung up.

I took my time filling the tank, and fussed with the window cleaning equipment I found next to the gas pumps. Ten minutes later, the sound of sirens filled the air as all sorts of vehicles went screaming past me. I don't care how many people Wish List has. Louisville Swat, LPD, the local media and bomb squad would be more than Rudy and his gang could handle all at once.

Knowing the scene was going to be pure bedlam for the next twenty-four hours, I figured I should get back to my woodland prisoners. But first I wanted to visit my former girlfriend, Rachel Case.

9.

RACHEL'S LIVE-IN HOUSEGUEST is my former psychiatrist, Dr. Nadine Crouch. Nadine is a retired psychotherapist who was originally hired by my government handlers to help me cope with losing three years of my life to a coma (don't ask, it's a long story). Nadine is a gifted, nononsense therapist, whose abrasive disposition is counterbalanced by the everpresent twinkle in her eye. She's mid to late sixties, slightly plump, and generally appealing in a gruff, spinster aunt sort of way. She's strong, capable, and the most mercenary human being you're likely to find on the planet. Sitting across the table, she was frowning, regarding me as she often did: with a sneer. But deep down, I know she's actually quite fond of me.

"Come to survey your work, Donovan?"

"My work?"

"Don't do that."

"Do what?"

"Don't repeat my words," she snapped. "I'm the shrink, not you."

I nodded. "You think I had something to do with Rachel's condition?"

"You think you didn't?"

"No. But I'm open to hearing your theory."

"Theory? That's rich. Fact: when you met her, Rachel had a husband, a house and a responsible job. Now she's a widow, homeless, and thinks she's Desmond Tutu."

"Desmond Tutu."

"That's what I said."

I shook my head. "First of all, Rachel's husband, Sam, was cheating on her. Second, she's not homeless. She owns this entire building, and could buy three more just like it. And third, she wouldn't know Desmond Tutu if he walked in wearing one. You're exaggerating again, Nadine."

"Maybe so. But you can't deny your part in all this."

"My part is I saved Rachel."

"From?"

I started to speak, but caught myself. This wasn't just me and Nadine sitting around, having a discussion about Rachel. She was probing me, pushing for a reaction. She was on the clock and I was being psychoanalyzed.

"Why don't you tell me how you see it?" I said.

She lifted an eyebrow. "I wouldn't want to say anything that might cost me my job."

"I've never known you to hold back an opinion."

She sighed. "I'm getting older, Donovan."

"You'll outlive us all."

"You, certainly. But I need to think of my future. Like my age, the cost of living continues to advance. I hate to think what might happen if I'm forced out onto the street at my age."

I laughed. "Nadine, you're a scary old miser. You're hoarding more than ten million dollars I personally know about, though I'm certain it's at least twice that, since I've never known you to pull so much as a penny from your purse. But please, speak freely. Your job is safe as long as Rachel wants you here."

"Well, that's comforting. Rachel's a dear girl, and despite

my meager wages, it's clear she needs me. Though I do worry about the two of you running off to start another crime spree."

"Oh, come on, Nadine. Rachel and I are great together."

"Oh, posh."

"Posh? Care to elaborate?"

"I dare not. Your fragmented identity poses an everpresent threat to my safety. I enjoy living these days, and I'd like to keep doing it awhile longer."

"You think I have it in me to kill you for expressing an opinion?"

"I do."

"Nadine, I'm shocked."

"You probably killed someone on the drive over here."

"Let's get back on subject," I said.

Nadine stood and walked to the small refrigerator on the other side of her office.

"Care for a bottled water?" she said.

"No thanks, I'm good."

She pulled out a single plastic bottle of water and handed it to me. It took me a moment to realize why.

"Arthritis acting up?"

Nadine shrugged. "We all have our weakness."

I twisted the cap open and handed the bottle back to her. "What's *my* weakness?"

"Simple. Rachel."

I thought about that a moment before saying, "How do you drink when I'm not here? Does Rachel open your bottles?"

She returned to her seat and took a sip. "I've got a special gripping thing I use."

We were quiet a moment.

"You really think Rachel's condition is my fault?"

Nadine said nothing.

"You can't deny she makes me a better person when we're together," I said.

She sipped her water. "You're old enough to be her father."

I waited.

"Fine," she said. "I won't deny it."

"Then what's the problem?"

"She brings out the best in you, even as you bring out the worst in her. But make no mistake, Donovan, you're a bad influence. The two of you were together for what, eight weeks this last time? And she killed a man?"

"She thought she was protecting me."

"Oh, please."

We were quiet again while Nadine sipped her water.

"How's Rachel now?" I asked.

Nadine shook her head while extending her palms in a gesture of frustration.

"She's like Starbucks," she said.

"Starbucks coffee?"

"Yeah, she's all over the place."

"Can you be more specific?"

"She's nuts!"

I frowned. "I thought you guys were opposed to that type of reference. You can't come up with any four-dollar words?"

"I keep my audience in mind before using technical terms."

"Funny."

"Look, Donovan, I know this is hard for you to believe, so let's take a stroll down memory lane. You didn't meet Rachel in a conventional way, did you?"

"Not really."

"In fact, you broke into her house and began living in her attic."

"To keep an eye on her husband."

"You remained there for two years."

"I'm thorough."

"You were fixated on Rachel."

"I wouldn't say fixated."

"Of course you wouldn't. But come on, Donovan. You built an elite video command center in her attic. You placed more than forty pinhole cameras throughout her house. From the garage to the bedroom to the toilet, you studied her every move, day and night. You invaded her privacy in the most personal and banal ways imaginable. It's perverted."

"You're making assumptions about my character and choice of viewing habits based on nothing more than the location of forty pinhole cameras."

Nadine studied me a moment, as if trying to decide whether I'd been angry, indignant, or simply making a point.

"Perhaps I am," she said.

"At any rate, watching Rachel didn't make her crazy. She didn't even know I was there."

"No she didn't. Until you told her."

"By then we were dating. I was being honest with her. You got a problem with honesty?"

"You gathered all this information about her—everything from her medications to her monthly cycle, to her arguments with Sam—and used it to seduce her."

"We were in love."

"You might have been in love, but for her it was complete and utter manipulation. To this day she waves to you in the ceiling of every room she enters. How would that make you feel to think someone was watching your every move?"

"Protected?"

Nadine sighed. "You're hopeless."

"Watching her didn't make her crazy."

She took another long drink of water. "It contributed. Of course, locking her away in a Lucite container, allowing her to think she could be killed at any moment, didn't help things."

"It was only two days. Anyway, I took her on vacation afterward."

"Mighty big of you, taking her to the beach after robbing and killing her husband."

"I didn't kill Sam."

"Really? So we can expect him to come waltzing in here someday? That's something I'd like to see."

"You like a good waltz, do you?"

She finished her water, then capped the empty bottle and placed it sideways on the table between us and flicked one end. It spun a few circles and came to a stop. She spun the bottle a few more times until it pointed at me. "I suppose you'll want to see her now?"

"Being such a bad influence, I'm surprised you'd permit it."

"What can I say? You sign my checks."

10.

"*KEVIN! OH, MY God!*"

Rachel had been lying on her bed when I came in. Now she jumped up and ran across the room and started hugging me so hard I nearly dropped her present.

"Hi honey," I said.

"You came to get me?"

"I came to visit."

She lifted her T-shirt all the way up to her neck. "Wanna feel my boobies?"

I did. But I doubted Nadine would approve.

"Later, maybe."

Rachel released her grip and her shirt fell back in place, ending the show like a Broadway curtain ends Act Three.

"You brought me an orchid plant!"

"White orchids still your favorite?"

"You know they are!"

"Then yes, I brought you an orchid plant."

"I love it! How long are you staying?"

"Not long enough."

"When you leave, can I go with you?"

"Of course. If that's what you want."

"What I want is a big kiss!"

I placed the orchid on the coffee table in her sitting area and we kissed like newlyweds. After awhile she took my hand

and led me to the edge of her bed, where we sat.

"I love you," she said.

"That makes me a lucky man."

"Say it."

"I love you, too."

"I thought I loved Sam, but then I met you."

"And this is better?"

She nodded.

"Can I ask you something?" she said.

"Of course."

"Did you kill Sam?"

"No."

"Promise? It's okay if you did, I just want to know."

"I promise."

A cloud passed over her face.

"What's wrong?" I said.

"Did I kill him?"

"No, of course not."

"Then Sam's alive?"

I didn't think so. After stealing all the money from Sam's clients', I left him with my associate, Callie Carpenter, who had expressed a strong desire to kill him. Callie was very good at killing, so I didn't hold out much hope for Sam's continued existence.

"Kevin?"

"Huh?"

"Is Sam alive?"

"I can't say for sure. Why all the questions about Sam?"

"You're the only one I know to ask. And Nadine says I need closure."

"If it turns out he's dead, would that help?"

She thought a moment. "Yup."

I took out my cell phone, called Callie, and asked if she'd heard from Sam recently. I listened a moment, then hung up and said, "Callie didn't kill him."

"So he's alive?"

"Far as I know."

Rachel nodded slowly. "Okay, then."

"You want me to find him?"

"Nope."

"Wouldn't be too hard to track him down."

"He can rot for all I care."

"Technically, he's still your husband."

"He's a lying, cheating prick."

He was indeed. However…

"Uh, you lied and cheated on Sam too," I said.

She looked at me through wide, sincere eyes and said, "That's different."

We looked at each other a moment, and she said, "You understand, don't you?"

I did. Most women believe their cheating is on a higher level than their husbands'because of the emotional connection they form with their lovers before having sex. Of course, I could argue that an emotional, physical affair is much worse than casual sex. But what do you expect me to say? I'm a guy.

"I do understand why it's different," I said.

She smiled brightly. "Thank you, Kevin."

Rachel knows my name is Donovan Creed, but she'd met me as Kevin Vaughn, and she's comfortable calling me that. I don't care what she calls me. Donovan Creed isn't my real name, either.

"Would you really take me with you?" she said.

"I'll take you right now if you want."

She paused. "Where are you going?"

"You mean from here? The first place?"

She nodded.

I took a deep breath. "Well, you might not believe this, but I've got a guy and a woman chained to trees in the woods in Southern Indiana. I have to set them free before we can actually do something fun. Oh, and I have to make sure another guy's wife doesn't get killed."

"Is she insane?"

"What?"

"Is she insane like me?"

I cupped her chin in my hand and looked into her tupelo honey-colored eyes. "You're not insane, Rachel. You're just wise in ways other people don't get."

"But you do."

"I do."

"And that's why you love me."

"It is."

"So this guy's wife. Why can't he keep her safe?"

"He's been kidnapped. But before that happened, he called me and said someone might try to kill his wife."

Rachel said, "Maybe you should take care of all that first, and then we can go somewhere together."

"That's probably a good idea."

I knew Rachel wouldn't leave her apartment. She was months away from being travel ready. But it's important for her to know that I'll always take care of her, whether she's with me on the road, or with Nadine in her million dollar penthouse.

We chatted a while longer, and then I left. After crossing the street I turned and looked for her in the window. She waved to me and I blew her a kiss. I continued standing where I was on the sidewalk, watching her in the window, and would have remained there an hour, had she continued to look at me.

The building that housed Rachel's penthouse apartment was actually a private hospital, though Rachel wasn't a patient. In fact, the nurses and psychiatrists who worked in the lower building were unaware she was receiving treatment. For all they knew, Rachel was Nadine's granddaughter, and they were living together, sharing the penthouse. So Rachel's "treatment" was unofficial, and I'm the one who set it up. I did so after learning Rachel killed a guy in Florida during our vacation. I thought it wise to get her out of the state as soon as possible and get Nadine involved, instead of the cops. So I used a portion of the funds I'd given Rachel to purchase an incomeproducing private hospital, where she could be quietly cared for by my former psychiatrist.

From her window, Rachel smiled and waved at me again. I gave her a full bow, and performed a little dance step. I'm a dreadful dancer, and my effort made her laugh.

Rachel had been here nearly four months, and shamefully, this was only my third visit. Each time I came she expressed an interest in leaving with me, and I always offered to take her. In the end, she always backed down.

My cell phone vibrated in my pocket. I retrieved it and smiled. With nothing more to go on than the caller ID, I knew who was behind Wish List:

My former associate, Victor.

This was going to be very interesting.

Rachel was still watching me from the window, so I waved again.

One day I'll show up and she'll be ready to run off on another wild adventure with me. Traveling with the moody, homicidal Rachel has its ups and downs. On the up side, she's incredibly sensual and tons of fun. On the down side, her violent mood swings are explosive, and could lead to murder.

Still, no one's perfect, and I enjoy her company more than any other woman I've known, which probably tells you something about me.

Up in the window, Rachel blew me a final kiss and closed the curtains. I stood there a moment longer, thinking about all the ways Rachel understands me that other women don't.

Take sex, for instance.

Rachel instinctively knows what type of sex I like most: frequent sex.

11.

"HAVE YOU...KILLED her?"

The voice on the other end of the line was tinny and labored, and came from a computer-generated voice program that belonged to Victor, the quadriplegic billionaire midget I'd worked with and killed for, several times.

"Killed who?" I said.

"Who...do you...think? Jinny...Kidwell."

"Is Hugo with you?" I asked. Of course he was. Hugo was always with Victor.

"I'll...put him on...speaker...phone." Victor said.

"Good. We can cover more ground that way."

Hugo said, "What's your interest in Buddy Pancake?"

Victor and Hugo are megalomaniacal midgets bent on world conquest. Victor is the brains and financier, Hugo is the general of their international army of little people. If Victor was involved, Wish List was another of his "Social Experiments." It was vintage Victor, granting desperate people four wishes, and then pulling the rug out from under them. A few years ago I'd been involved with another of Victor's social experiments. He'd been offering financially strapped people a hundred thousand dollars if they agreed to let him kill a criminal who had never paid for his crime. Of course, in Victor's mind, by taking the money they'd become accessories. It was my job to assassinate them. I didn't get very far before my conscience got the better of me. Considering the magnitude of evil they've unleashed upon the world, Victor and Hugo have somehow managed to keep—pardon the pun—a low profile in the criminal world.

"Must I repeat the question?" Hugo said.

"My interest in Buddy Pancake? I want to save his life."

"Why?"

"I owe his sister."

"Who's his sister?"

"It's complicated."

"Is Jinny Kidwell alive?"

"How would I know?"

"What are your plans for her?

"What makes you think I even know her?"

Hugo sighed. "Our cameras picked you up in Buddy's garage. If you know about Buddy you know about Wish List. If you know about Wish List you know about his connection to Jinny Kidwell. Early this morning we learned that Jinny Kidwell was missing from her trailer. That means someone snuck past ten highly trained perimeter guards and removed her from the premises without making a sound, something no one on earth could have managed. Except you."

"You consider those guys highly trained?"

"It's what I was led to believe. In any event, what are your plans with regard to Ms. Kidwell?"

"I'm going to exchange her for Buddy."

"Easily done. Is she alive?"

"Is he?"

"At the moment, I believe he is."

"When last I saw her, Jinny was alive as well."

"Where is she?"

"Where's Buddy?"

"Look, Mr. Creed. Jinny is one of the highest profile people in the world. If she remains missing, or dies, there will be endless media coverage. Victor's plans could be compromised."

"If you can't handle the pressure, you shouldn't have accepted Jinny's wishes."

"You don't understand. We're trying to save her life."

"I fail to see how paying Buddy Pancake a million dollars for a roll in the hay could possibly save her life."

"That's the payment she had to make to stay alive. And a damn small one, I think you'll agree."

"What's wrong with her?"

"She's kept it quiet for months, but she's got an incurable disease."

"And you've got an antidote?"

"We do."

"Then what's the problem?"

"It's one dose."

"What, you can't make more?"

"The chemist died in an accident. His formula died with him. Our people have spent the past ten months trying to analyze it a drop at a time. We've made progress, but we're years away. Unfortunately, the serum breaks down over time, and when that happens the components can't be analyzed. The shelf life is short, less than a year, and we're closing in on that deadline. We've done all we can, but it's over. We can't duplicate or replace it. But we *can* save Jinny's life. She's had three injections, but needs one more, and she needs it today, if possible. Bottom line, there's only enough serum left for one dose."

"And you promised it to Jinny?"

"That's right."

"What's the disease?"

He paused. "I can't tell you."

"Why not? My line's secure."

"So is ours. But Victor hasn't authorized me to tell you."

"Victor?" I said. "Hello?"

"He's not here."

"He left the room? I didn't hear his wheelchair."

"It's a brand new one. Completely silent."

"Does he ever creep up on you?"

"All the time. Scares the shit out of me."

"What's he doing right now?"

"Meeting with our computer programmer."

"Can you interrupt him?"

"Not a good idea."

"Fair enough. I'll ask him when I see him. In the meantime, tell me about Buddy, starting with where he is right now."

"Arizona."

"Jinny's in Indiana," I said, letting him know I'll be more specific when he is.

"He's in a ranch house that borders twenty thousand acres of private land."

"Why?"

"He's a participant in a hunting game."

"Against his will?"

"I'd say so."

"What's the game?"

"They call it 'Run, Son!'"

"Never heard of it."

"There are a dozen hunters with rifles, and Buddy and forty-nine other Wish List alumni are prey. They'll have a two-hour head start, but they won't escape."

"Why's that?"

"They've had monitoring devices planted in their backs, next to their spines, where they can't reach them."

"What if Buddy gets one of the other participants to dig it out?"

"It'll explode, rendering him paralyzed."

"Like Victor."

"Except that Victor won't be lying on the desert floor, helpless, when the hunters come."

"Tell me the rest of it."

"There's a point system. As prey, Buddy's worth seventy points to the hunter that bags him. The younger, stronger, faster targets are worth up to 250 points. When the last kill is made, the points are totaled and the winners receive valuable prizes."

"How do you verify the points?"

"The hunters dig the devices out of their backs."

"Each device is labeled with the points?"

"Correct."

"You think Buddy's head will wind up mounted on someone's wall?"

"I think we'll bury him with the others deep in the desert after the point count, unless you return Jinny to us. Where is she?"

"I left her chained to a tree in the woods."

"Her health won't permit it. You've got to get her to us immediately."

"I can do that. Provided you spare Buddy's life."

"Buddy's worth squat. There's got to be a catch."

"I also want you to leave his wife alone. Forever."

"Will that do it?"

"Nearly."
"What else?"
"They get to keep the million dollars."
"Done."

12.

WHEN JINNY KIDWELL and Harrison Ford heard me coming they broke into excited stage whispers. Poor things, that's all the vocal power they had left. Had I been searching a hundred yards away instead of knowing their exact location, I would have missed them.

As I made my way through the underbrush, their pleas became more urgent. But upon seeing me, they grew silent.

Jinny didn't look as frail as I expected, but she was pissed. She unleashed a torrent of curses at me like none I'd ever heard from a woman. And I've known some tough women! But curses are more effective with volume, and Jinny's invectives, though scathing, came across as comical.

I tried not to smile. She caught me and began another round.

"Relax, Jinny," I said. "You're about to be saved."

Calling over my shoulder, I said, "You too, Harrison. Hang on. I'll be there in a minute. You'll be back with your wife before you know it."

Jinny's steel wrist band was secured to a length of chain that wound around the tree. When I circled the tree to remove the chain I noticed something on the ground.

"Is that yours?"

She turned to look at me and followed my stare. Then she stopped cursing and lowered her head, embarrassed.

"I'll be damned," I said, grinning.

"A gentleman would pretend not to notice my droppings," she whispered. Then she grew angry again and whisper-shouted, "What the hell's *wrong* with you?"

"I was just trying to calculate what that might be worth on eBay, if I could get it documented."

It took her a moment to process my words. Then she whispered, "*What?*"

"Scarlett Johansson blew her nose into a handkerchief and sold it for fifty-three hundred dollars. The same buyer paid twenty-eight thousand for a half-eaten grilled cheese sandwich."

"That's disgusting. *You're* disgusting!"

"I suppose I could get one of those DNA testing labs to authenticate it. They might certify it came from you."

"You're *joking!*"

I *was* joking. But not about the value of Jinny Kidwell's scat in today's celebrity-crazed society. I had no doubt that her droppings would fetch a hundred grand, if marketed properly.

Really, I'm kidding. I mean, about actually doing it.

Later, in the car heading south, after two hours of angry silence and a couple of hot teas with honey and lemon, Jinny's voice was on the mend. She was hoarse, but I could understand her.

"Did you even stop to think about us?"

"What do you mean?"

"If something had happened to you, we would have died out there."

"I told someone where you were."

"You did?"

"Not the exact location, but yes, in general."

"I doubt that."

"No, really. I told my girlfriend."

She appeared, not surprised, but stunned. "You've got a girlfriend?"

"I do."

"For real?"

"Of course."

"What's her name?"

"Rachel."

Jinny shook her head, sadly.

"What's the matter?" I said.

"She'd have to be insane."

13.

I CONTINUED DRIVING south, through Nashville, and eventually dropped Jinny and me off at a private airstrip near Franklin, Tennessee. Before boarding our charter jet, I untied Harrison, returned his car keys, and gave him a generous tip, along with a warning that I was counting on his complete discretion. Jinny showed her sweet side by giving him a long hug and thanking him for helping her get through their ordeal. Then Jinny and I climbed in the Hawker 400 XP and flew to the remote landing strip near Great Bend, Kansas, where the exchange would be made. Hugo and I were in constant contact during the flight, and he caught me up to speed on everything that had happened in Buddy's miserable life since filling out the form on wishlist.bz.

Upon landing, I told Jinny and the pilots to remain on-board and visible. Then I walked, as instructed, to the fourth hangar, and knocked on the door.

"Face the wall while I pat you down," said one of Victor's huge, well-muscled goons.

I looked at Hugo and said, "Is this really necessary?"

He shrugged. "Sorry. Try to take it as a compliment."

I endured it.

"He's clean," the goon said.

"I can guarantee you, he's armed." Hugo said.

The goon looked down at Hugo with scorn. "You tellin'

me my job, little man?"

"Maybe you two should get a room," I said.

"Maybe I should stuff my foot up your ass!"

"You'll have to buy me dinner first."

"Where's the weapon?" Hugo said.

I pointed to the watch on my left wrist.

Hugo nodded.

"The fuck is that?" said the goon.

"Wireless detonator."

"Bullshit," he said. "You haven't had time to wire this place."

Hugo shook his head. "The plane, stupid."

"Why would he blow up the—oh. *Shit!*"

I sighed. "Hugo. Can we get this thing done?"

We walked into the hanger and up to a Lear 45 where I saw Buddy Pancake's face in one of the windows.

"Why's he making that stupid face?" said Hugo.

"I think he's trying to signal me that someone's holding a gun on him."

"Like you wouldn't have figured *that* out."

The goon stopped near the exit door of the jet, and Hugo and I kept walking toward the office in the back of the hangar. As I passed, I nodded at Buddy to let him know I got his message. Buddy kept mouthing the words, "They've got guns! Guns!"

Hugo said, "What a moron."

I said, "Jinny Kidwell for this guy? Gotta be the worst hostage trade in history."

Hugo laughed.

A voice behind me said, "Hello, Donovan."

I knew the voice. I turned.

"I'll be damned," I said.

"Yes you will."

It was Rachel's husband.

"What have you been up to, Sam?"

Sam said, "You know. Just livin'the dream." Then he said, "You still banging my wife?"

"Not so much."

"Can't say I blame her."

There were dark circles under Sam's eyes. His face had a pasty pallor, and his hair was unkempt. He sounded bitter, and looked five years older than he should. I'm sure it's hard being Sam, a lonely computer genius with no family, friends, or peers in his profession.

"Rachel was asking about you," I said.

"When?"

"Earlier today."

"And what did you say?"

I shrugged. "What's there to say?"

He nodded. "Do I have any chance with her at all? Your honest opinion."

I said, "The Wish List computer program. Is that your work?"

"You like it?"

"I admire the effort."

"Do you have any inkling how impressive an achievement that is? I mean, can you even comprehend the magnitude of what I put together?"

I didn't. But based on his question I figured it must be pretty damn special. I said, "It's sheer genius."

"It's child's play," he said.

I shrugged. "Victor hired you to create it?"

"Wouldn't you?"

"I would. You're the best computer person I've ever known."

He shook his head. "You have no idea." Then he muttered something about how the rest of us are mere insects trying to fathom quantum physics.

Then he walked away.

14.

VICTOR WAS SITTING in the front office in his space age wheelchair, flanked by two little people half my size who I regarded as more dangerous than the goon outside.

"Hugo…tells me…that…Jinny's alive."

"She is."

"Then…let's…make the…trade."

Victor's metallic voice is creepy enough on the phone. In person it's unearthly.

I said, "What's wrong with Jinny?"

"She's got…AIDS."

"Jesus."

"Exactly."

"And you've got a cure?"

"One…dose."

"Damn."

"Exactly."

"Look, Victor, you can't just tell me some guy, working alone, discovered a cure for AIDS. He's got no notes? Give me a break. That's not how these things work in real life."

"Why…do you…care?"

"I might want to write a book someday. You think my readers are going to accept that type of bullshit explanation?"

"You…haven't…even…written a…book but…you're worried…about…what your… readers are…going…to think?"

"Yeah, that's right."

"Well if...you...write...a book..."

"Yeah?"

"Keep me...out of it."

"You'll change your mind when we shoot the movie version."

"Who...do you...think they'll...get to...play me...in...the movie?"

I thought about it a minute, then gave up. "Victor, you're an original. They'll have to pay through the nose to get you to play yourself. You'll have them over a barrel."

He seemed pleased about the movie role, so I got back to it. "So what happened? Tell me about the doctor."

Victor motioned to Hugo to speak, which is what he did whenever too many words needed to be said. Using the respirator to generate his computer voice for more than a few sentences was not only time consuming, but exhausting for Victor.

Hugo said, "His name was Gero Mielke."

"German?"

"Correct."

"What was his specialty?"

Hugo shrugged. "Microbiology, virology, blood cancer specialist..." His voice trailed off.

"Working alone?"

"When we met him he was director of the Berlin Mutational Virology Laboratory. He led his team to the edge of what he realized was a breakthrough, then moved them in a different direction and continued the work alone."

"Why?"

"He wanted to cash in."

"How much did you offer?"

"He was going to sell us the formula for a billion dollars."

"Beats a salary bump at the lab, I'll bet."

"Exactly."

We were all quiet for a moment. I spoke first. "You're positive Jinny's got AIDS?"

"Yes," said Hugo. "One hundred percent. But it's nearly cured."

"And her husband?"

"HIV positive."

"But not AIDS?"

"Not yet."

"And Buddy?"

"I'm afraid Buddy will be dead by December."

"But how is that possible? AIDS doesn't kill that quickly."

"Apparently the serum that is saving Jinny accelerates the disease in her sexual partners. Dr. Mielke learned that during the testing phase."

"So Jinny knew she was killing Buddy by sleeping with him?"

"Of course."

I shook my head. "And she called *me* disgusting!"

"Women, right?" Hugo said.

"But why isn't Jinny's husband dead by now?"

"She and Pete haven't had sex since learning about her condition."

An interesting thought came into my mind. "If Jinny gets cured, will she kill all her future sexual partners?"

"No one knows."

"What about Buddy's wife, Lissie?"

"What about her?"

"Has he infected her?"

"No. There's been no sexual contact between them since

he's been with Jinny."

"Good thing," I said.

Then I thought of something else. "Who infected Jinny Kidwell?"

"Her husband."

"What?"

"He was cheating on Jinny and wound up with HIV. He didn't contract the disease, but he became a carrier, and passed it on to Jinny."

"I was wondering why he allowed her to fuck Buddy Pancake."

"Now you know. So, are you ready to make the trade?"

"There are what, twenty, thirty million people living with AIDS?"

"More like forty-five million. And five million new cases a year."

"A billion dollars seems cheap. What happened, you got greedy?"

"No. We made several payments, but Dr. Mielke began making impossible demands. In the end, he was a raging paranoid who thought we were going to steal his formula. He tore up his notes and worked alone at night, after his team left the lab. He began missing our deadlines and refused to continue working without being paid. The situation got out of hand."

"What happened to him?"

Hugo and Victor exchanged a look. Hugo said, "Unfortunately, Dr. Mielke died before we could resolve our issues."

"Cause of death?"

"Heart attack."

"Uh huh. Was there torture involved?"

Victor said, "A little."

"You thought you might be able to force his cooperation."

Hugo said, "The idea made sense at the time."

"But you tortured him to death."

"Not me, but yes, that was the unhappy result."

"The man was living a double life."

"Yes."

"Working day and night, the guilt, the stress...your people should have known."

"True."

"Torture is an exact science, better left to professionals."

"So we've learned."

"You should have called me."

Victor smiled. "Next time."

15.

AFTER MAKING THE trade, Buddy and I climbed in the Hawker and strapped on the seat belts.

"What about the device in my back?" he said.

"Is it uncomfortable?"

"What do *you* think? They dug a hole in my back and stuck a piece of metal in there."

"What are you taking for it?"

"They gave me Dilaudid tablets. Said they have two to eight times the painkilling effects of morphine." He looked at me. "Is that true?"

"How would I know? I don't use pain pills."

"Why not?"

"They keep you from feeling pain, right?"

He didn't know how to respond, so he said, "Can you believe those bastards did this to me? Now I'm going to need surgery to dig that thing out."

"You'd better use one of my contacts. Otherwise it'll be reported."

"Fine. I *want* it to be reported. They were going to hunt me down, shoot me like a fuckin' animal. I'm going straight to the cops. I'll bring those assholes to their *knees*!"

The co-pilot turned around in his chair and looked at me. "Everything all right?"

I nodded. Then said, "Buddy, look at me."

When he did, I said, "You're not going to tell anyone about this."

"What? Why the hell not?"

"Because for once in your life you're going to do the right thing."

"What's *that* supposed to mean?"

"I promised the Wish List people you'd keep your mouth shut."

"Why?"

"So they wouldn't kill your wife."

He went quiet awhile, but not long enough to suit me. "You really think they'd kill Lissie?" he said.

"I guarantee it."

"But you could stop them."

"I just did."

"But only if I say nothing."

"You got it. Finally."

We landed in Richmond, and I said goodbye to the pilots and got a rental car. Buddy's back was getting worse, so I took a look at it.

"It's infected," I said.

"I'm not surprised. Hurts like a sonovabitch."

"Don't worry about the seatbelt." I buckled it to keep it from dinging, and he sat on it. I fired up the car and pulled onto I-64 heading west. "The news gets worse, Buddy."

"What could be worse than the past few days?"

"You're dying."

"What? No! It's just an infection. Look, take me to Jewish Hospital, and drop me off. I've got great insurance."

"Buddy, we're in Richmond, Virginia, not Louisville. I'm driving you to a private facility that houses the finest surgeons in the world."

"Mr. Creed, really, you've done more than I could have hoped for. I mean, Jesus, you saved my life. So please. Don't worry about me. Or Lissie. We'll be fine, I promise. I'm no Donovan Creed, but I can take it from here."

"You're not listening to me. You're dying."

"Look. I'm not a tough guy, we both know that. But this is just a simple surgical procedure."

"If it's not removed properly, the device in your back will detonate and blow out your spine."

"Excuse me?"

I pulled off at the next exit, found an abandoned Popeye's Fried Chicken restaurant, and parked behind it.

"I'm taking you to Sensory Resources, a branch of Homeland Security. There are surgeons there who can take that thing out of your back tonight. But you need to understand, after this, things will never be the same."

"What do you mean?"

"You're dying. And not because of the device."

"What are you talking about?"

"You've got fullblown AIDS, Buddy."

He laughed. "Right."

"I'm serious. Ever ask yourself why Jinny Kidwell paid you a million dollars and let you have sex with her?"

"Of course. So I asked her."

"And she gave you that bullshit story about paying back into the system?"

He nodded.

"Jinny Kidwell has AIDS. She heard about Wish List, filled out the form, and asked for a cure for AIDS."

"They've got a cure for AIDS? Who *are* these guys?"

"The kind of guys who began giving her the treatments, and told her if she wanted to complete them she'd have to perform some tasks."

"Like fucking me."

"And paying a million dollars."

"Are you honestly trying to tell me that I have AIDS?"

"I am."

"Mr. Creed, AIDS doesn't work like that. You get HIV first. Then, years later, if you're unlucky, you *might* get AIDS."

"I'm not familiar with the normal progression of the disease. But it doesn't matter in your case because the injections they gave Jinny caused you to acquire the disease, and accelerate its progression at an abnormal pace. I've been told by a very reliable source that you'll be dead by December."

"You swear to God?"

"It's true."

"Swear it. Swear to God."

"What are we, eight years old?"

"What about the antidote? If they gave it to Jinny, they can give it to me. I'll do whatever it takes. Call them. I've still got the million. I'll pay it. Tell them. Tell them I'll have sex with anyone they say."

"You really think someone's going to put having sex with you on their wish list?"

"That was just a for instance. I'll do whatever. Please, just call them. Tell them I'll do whatever they want. I'll kill someone. Hell, I'll kill ten people. Babies, if they want. I'll—"

"Shut up, Buddy. Babies? Jesus. Anyway, there's no more serum. There was only one batch ever made, and the guy who invented it died, leaving no records behind. Only one patient will ever receive the treatment, and that's Jinny Kidwell. And you, Mr. I'll Do Anything, Even Kill Ten Babies—are shit out of luck."

Buddy began sobbing. The harder he sobbed, the worse his

back hurt. Which made him yell. Then he sobbed some more, which made him yell again, and this went on for more than a minute until I finally said, "Wind it up, will you?"

"What's to become of me?"

"You're going to die. Get over it, you miserable fuck."

"What about Lissie?"

"If it's true you haven't had sex with her, she'll be all right physically."

"I need to tell her. I need to explain things."

"If you do, they'll kill her."

"Why?"

"Think about it. Jinny Kidwell, the world's most famous actress, is about to be cured of AIDS. If word gets out, the entire world will change. Desperate people do desperate things, and people will demand answers. The easiest way to prevent that is to kill everyone who can't keep a secret. Starting with you, and then Lissie. Then both sets of relatives, and all your friends."

"That's crazy. They'll never get away with it."

"They won't have to, because it's not going to come to that."

"Why not?"

"Because you're never going to see Lissie again. You're not going to see anyone again. You're going to be isolated from all human contact, save for the doctors and nurses who'll be taking care of you in a secluded treatment facility."

"That's ridiculous."

"Maybe so, but that's the plan."

"What about the money?"

"Lissie will get half."

"You're still planning to take half my money? It's all I have left!"

"I'm donating your half to the doctors and nurses at Sensory who will be keeping you comfortable as the disease progresses. By the time you die, I'll have put together an elaborate explanation for why you went missing, and how you died a hero. Better to have Lissie remember you as a hero than to learn you got AIDS cheating on her. Don't you agree?"

"No. I want to talk to her. Lissie's a good person. If I explain everything, she'll forgive me."

"You think she'll be okay with getting raped by your best friend?"

He paused. "I'll skip over that part. She'll forgive the rest."

"You're going to be an invalid. You think that's fair?"

"She loves me."

"Have you heard a word I've said?"

"Of course I have. But the bottom line is I only care about Lissie. I don't give a damn what happens to anyone else."

I sighed. "Maybe I should just kill you now."

"Maybe you should," Buddy said, "but you won't. My sister loved you. She said you were a violent man, but a good one. You know that what happened to me wasn't fair. You might not protect me from here on out, but you'll let me end things on my own terms."

16.

BUDDY DIDN'T KNOW me as well as he thought.

After snapping his neck I drove his body to my former headquarters in Carroll County, Virginia, and told the medical team that Buddy Pancake's body was racked with a mutated AIDS virus that had been contracted through sexual intercourse with a woman who had received a treatment that was said to cure AIDS. I suggested that by performing detailed tests on his body, they might be able to backtrack their way into a cure for AIDS. It was a long shot, but what the hell. Buddy's life might as well stand for something positive.

I spent the night in my old bunk at Sensory. The next morning I put Buddy's wallet, clothing, lower jaw, and personal effects in plastic bags, stuffed the bags in a big laundry bag, and headed back to the Richmond airport. From there I flew by private jet to Cincinnati, where I met my old friend and sometime employer, Sal Bonadello, crime boss for the Midwestern United States. Sal charged me a hundred grand to fake Buddy's death in a convincing way. Then I rented a car and drove to Louisville, broke into Buddy's garage, gathered up his million dollars, and took it back to Cincinnati. Caught another private flight back to Chicago, and got a good night's sleep.

A few weeks after Buddy's funeral, I had Callie Carpenter pay a visit to Lissie and present her with a check for a million dollars. Sporting the credentials of a real, live insurance executive, Callie explained that this sum represented the proceeds from an accidental death policy Buddy had quietly taken out years ago.

"This check is from an attorney," Lissie said.

"We always escrow the funds with a law firm while we investigate our claims. It shows good faith on our part, and makes a difference in the courtroom if a claim is denied."

"Well, I don't know what to say," Lissie said, "except to thank you, and your company. As I said, I didn't even know about the policy until you called."

"It's a shock to you, but we see this happen all the time," Callie said.

The attorney didn't exist, but the account did, and Lissie was happy enough with the unexpected windfall not to dig too deeply into the details. I mean, would you?

Buddy had always been a loose cannon and I should have known from the beginning that saving him was a lost cause. I owed his sister Lauren big time, but I think even she would agree that her brother was a toad of a man.

He did have great taste in women, though.

Jinny Kidwell?

Are you kidding me?

And Lissie?

Wow!

EPILOGUE

ALTHOUGH VICTOR'S PEOPLE came through for Jinny Kidwell and administered the serum, it didn't take. She's no longer with us, as you know (unless you're from another galaxy). Even then you'd know, since her funeral was beamed to space satellites and viewed by more than a hundred and ninety million people around the world.

She's now known as "The Face of AIDS," and her posters can be found at every rally.

The doctors at Sensory were unable to extract anything useful from Buddy's body to produce a cure for AIDS, and the disease has now surpassed bubonic plague to become the fifth leading epidemic in the history of the world.

Buddy has been dead for six months, and Lissie finally decided to move on with her life after meeting a great guy at the local community college where her support group meets every Tuesday night. His name is Matt Pike, and weeks into the meetings, when they finally got together for coffee, he somehow managed to rekindle feelings inside her that had been dormant since Buddy passed. He's not only handsome and charming, he seems to know her every thought and emotion, which he proved by allowing their relationship to progress at a comfortable pace. He's a keeper, the most thoughtful man she's ever met. I know all this because I listen in on her phone calls.

Last Tuesday Lissie finally agreed to meet Matt for dinner tonight at Z's. I worry what he might try to do afterward, when he brings her back home. She's vulnerable and he's smooth, a bad combination. Lou Kelly performed an extensive background check on him and everything came back clean. Moreover, Matt seems to be a decent guy. Still, I wonder if I should have let things get this far.

One of the things Lissie and her friends like best about Matt is that he's not in a rush to get her clothes off.

I like that about him too, and I hope that trend continues.

But I worry.

He's a man, and like I say, she's vulnerable. So I'll be watching their every move from my command center in Lissie's attic. This afternoon when Lissie came home, I saw that she'd bought several sets of sexy bras and panties. I watched her try them on, watched her check herself out in the mirror. She's looking fine and knows it, and I'm happy for her.

I know what you're thinking, but you're wrong. This isn't voyeurism. Sure, I've seen Lissie naked hundreds of times while living in her attic these many months. But that's not why I'm here. Not entirely.

I originally moved in because I wanted to keep an eye on Lissie, to make sure none of the Wish People came back to bother her. I was particularly concerned about Rudy and Perkins, the limo driver. These two would know Lissie was alone, and I couldn't bear to leave her unprotected. I knew going in that Victor's people had installed a number of high-quality pinhole cameras in the ceilings, but I expanded the grid to cover every square inch of the premises.

And I've watched over her ever since.

To, you know, make sure she was safe.

But over the days and weeks that followed, I found myself

becoming more and more attracted to this precious creature. The hardest part was watching her cry herself to sleep every night, knowing her tears were being wasted on a hapless loser like Buddy. But grief is something that has to run its course, so I spent those nights lying on the attic floor, ten feet above her bed, wishing there was something I could do to comfort her.

Then Matt came along. In many ways, he's been her salvation.

But again, I worry what might happen.

I'm depraved. Victor and Hugo are possibly worse, Rachel's crazy, Nadine's a mercenary skinflint, Rudy, Perkins and Sal Bonadello are gangsters, Lou Kelly's a killer, Pete was a philanderer, Jinny was morally bankrupt, Buddy was slime, and his old, lonely neighbor shits himself.

The point is I don't get to meet many saints in my line of work.

But Lissie's one.

How Buddy managed to win her is beyond my ability to comprehend, but it puts me in mind of something my grandfather once said: "Only a woman can look at a sack of shit and see a husband inside."

Rudy surfaced.

He showed up at Lissie's a couple nights ago. I saw him casing her house from across the street for over an hour. I didn't do anything about it. "Live and let live," I always say. In fact, I didn't kill him until he tried to enter through the garage.

I'm here for Lissie. And for now, I'm allowing Matt to be a part of her life. I just hope he doesn't do anything to spoil my trust.

There aren't many sincere gifts a guy like me can give a

woman like Lissie, though she deserves so much after what she's been through. I'm giving her the gift of my protection, which of course is insignificant compared to what she gave Buddy.

She gave him her love.

What greater gift can anyone give?

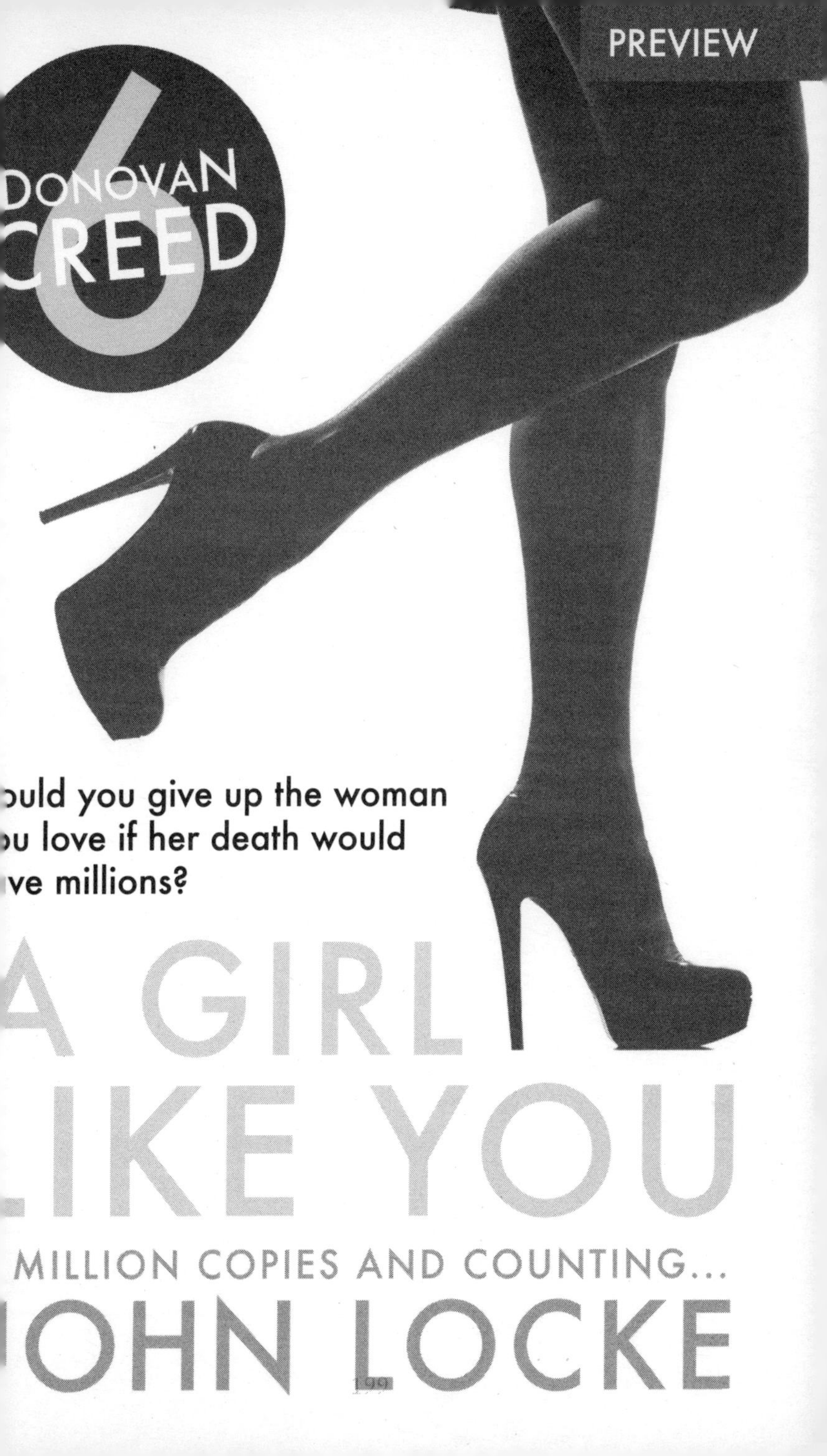
PREVIEW
6
DONOVAN
CREED
ould you give up the woman
ou love if her death would
ve millions?
A GIRL
LIKE YOU
MILLION COPIES AND COUNTING...
OHN LOCKE

PROLOGUE

MOST PEOPLE WOULD think getting bit on the balls by a water moccasin while sitting on the toilet in their own home would be the worst thing that could happen that day.

Sam Case knew better.

After hopping around like a Zuni Indian rain dancer and shrieking himself hoarse, Sam called 911. The dispatcher, a young man with a velvety voice named Earl—Please—Calm—Down—Sir—I'm—Only—Trying—To—Help—You, tried to make sense of Sam's call. It wasn't working, but Earl had the good sense to tell Sam to unlock his front door.

Sam did, then passed out.

Hours later in Brightside Hospital, Sam pressed the button on the morphine pump and turned his attention to the detectives standing at his bedside.

"Did you catch the snake?" Sam said.

"Not our job," one of them said.

"You're going to what, leave it there?"

"Don't you have a housekeeper or something?" the other one said.

Sam glanced at the second detective. Maybe it was the angle, or the drugs, or the hospital lighting—but the guy appeared to have no eyebrows. Was that possible? He fixed his gaze on the man's face.

"What happened to your eyebrows?"

"Fuck my eyebrows," he snarled.

Sam frowned. "You can't just walk around with no eyebrows and expect people not to pose the question."

The first detective chuckled.

"You think that's funny?" the second one said.

"Sorry, Gene. But yeah, it's funny."

Sam said, "A job like yours, you must encounter children."

Gene said, "So?"

"Kids are honest. They say what's on their mind. What do you tell them when they recoil in horror and shriek, "Oh, dear God! What happened to your fucking eyebrows?"

Gene's face reddened. "Listen, asshole. We can either be friends or I can use your nuts as a speed bag. Which sounds better to you?"

"One would be as unpleasant as the other," Sam said.

"Relax, both of you," the first detective said.

"Who are you?" Sam said to the less-creepy detective. "And why are you here?"

"I'm Gene Brightside," he said, then nodded at the other guy. "My partner, Gene Caruso." Caruso showed Sam his middle finger and mouthed the words "fuck you." What Caruso lacked in eyebrows he made up for with an honest-to-God Frito Bandito mustache. Where Brightside sported a navy suit with a red tie and matching pocket square, Caruso had on a brown T-shirt, black leather jacket, and wore a pair of faded Levi's covered in cat hair.

"Fatty acid supplement," Sam said.

"What?"

"You need to upgrade your cat's diet. A pet's coat is a reflection of what it eats."

"What makes you think I have a cat?"

Sam pointed to Caruso's pants. "You've got half a cat. The

rest of it is on your pants."

Caruso looked down at his legs, then back at Sam and said, "Fuck you, Case!"

"Digestible protein," Sam said. "And a fatty acid supplement. Your pet will thank you. Once that's taken care of, maybe we can work on your wardrobe, Superfly."

"How'd you know it was a water moccasin?" Brightside said.

"What?"

"You're in Louisville, Kentucky."

"So?"

"You don't find many water moccasins in this area."

"No shit," Sam said. Then added, "Shouldn't you be asking me how a snake got in my toilet in the first place?"

"You get a good look at the snake?"

Sam studied Detective Brightside's face. "I take Lunesta," he said.

"Lunesta."

"Yeah, that's right. To help me sleep."

Detective Brightside looked at Caruso, then back at Sam. "What's that got to do with the snake?"

"Lunesta works best in a dark room. When I get up in the middle of the night to piss, I keep the lights off. I sit on the toilet to keep from spraying piss on the floor."

"Fascinating," Caruso said.

"Four o'clock this morning, I get up to take a piss. In the dark. I walk from the bed to the master bath..."

"How far is the bed from the master bath?" Brightside said.

"Eleven steps," Sam said. "Twenty-eight-point-six feet."

The Genes looked at each other. "You believe this guy?" Caruso said.

"He's precise," Brightside said. "I'll give him that."

"You want to hear the story or what?" Sam said.

"Please," Brightside said. "Go on."

"I sit on the toilet, start pissing, and suddenly there's a white-hot pain in my nuts. I try to jump up, but can't."

"Why not?"

"Because of the three foot snake attached to my ball sack."

"How'd you know it was three feet long?"

"I reached between my legs and pulled the mother-fucker out of the toilet. Squeezed him hard enough to make him detach his fangs. When he did, I slammed his body against the wall two, three times. Then I flung him on the floor and turned on the lights. It was a water moccasin."

"You kill him?"

"No. He slithered away." Sam looked at Brightside. "How convenient, right?"

Brightside said, "This hospital was named after my father, Robin Brightside."

"That's a random thing to say."

"I just meant if there's anything you need, I'll personally ask the staff."

Sam said, "If your family's that wealthy, how'd you wind up a detective?"

"The old man died and left all his money to a bimbo. But the staff is sympathetic to me. Again, anything you need, I can help you."

"Thanks. I'll let you know."

Brightside nodded.

Caruso said, "Did it hurt? Getting your nut sack bit by a water moccasin?"

Sam gave him a withering look.

Brightside said, "The police did a walk through while you

were on the way to the hospital. According to them, all the doors and windows were locked, except the front door."

"I unlocked the front door so the paramedics could get in."

"After the snake bit you?"

Sam said, "Are you really that stupid? Or are you just fucking with me?"

Brightside said, "I was wondering why the alarm didn't go off when you opened the door."

Sam's look made it apparent he hadn't considered that fact. "I must've forgot to set it that night."

"You have any idea who put a snake in your toilet?" Brightside finally asked.

Sam knew exactly who put it there.

And why.

But what he said was, "I have no idea."

1.

24 Hours Earlier...

THE NYAC IS widely considered the world's greatest athletic club. Located at 180 Central Park South, the 21-story structure boasts 300 guest rooms, a boxing ring, swimming pool, billiards room that overlooks the park, two handball courts, and a number of meeting rooms. The exterior is limestone and concrete, crafted with an Italian Renaissance influence.

When I'm in the city, that's where I go to work out. You want to find me, come early. Ask for Donovan Creed.

Today I'm miles away from the NYAC. I'm across town, in the financial district, standing in front of The New York Gentlemen's Gym. The NYGG is twice as plush as the NYAC, if you can just imagine. I'm wearing olive cargo pants and a Dri-Fit training tee, carrying the vintage leather gym bag that had been used on at least one occasion by the Manassa Mauler himself, Jack Dempsey.

Upon entering, the first thing I see is two security guys in the lobby, talking. I stand a few feet away from them and wait politely till they're finished. Short, wide guy with a hand-stitched tapered shirt is younger, with a no-nonsense air of aggression. He looks me over, sizing me up.

"Need somethin'?" He says.

"Billy King here yet?"

He looks me up and down a second time, then looks at his friend.

Short, wide guy juts his chin toward the double doors.

"Boxing ring's in there," he says. "Billy's in it, poundin' turds outta some poor sap."

I nod.

There's a check-in area, but no one's manning the station.

Second security guy is older, maybe fifty. He's average height, lanky, weighs half as much as his muscle-bound friend. His eyes are kindly, and blue, and framed by ancient scar tissue. In a fair fight between them, my money's on the older guy.

He looks at my gym bag.

"That's a hell of a nice bag," he says. "A classic."

The three of us stand there, looking at my classic gym bag.

Older guy says, "Mind if I have a look inside?"

"What's your name?" I say.

"Does it matter?"

"The police might want a statement later on. I don't want to have to refer to you as 'young guy'and 'older guy.'"

"That's funny," older guy says.

"Why's that?"

"My name's Guy," he says.

"No shit?"

"Swear to God."

"Now there's a coincidence."

"And you are?"

"Donovan Creed."

I look at the young guy. He says, "What?"

"Your name," Guy says.

"Why does he care?" Younger guard says.

"I might need a witness later," I say.

He shrugs. He's so muscle bound, the simple effort of lifting his shoulders nearly doubles the volume of his neck.

"You can call me Z."

"Z," I say.

"That's right."

"That your street name?"

"You got a problem with that?"

Z and I are looking at each other, but out of the corner of my eye I see Guy roll his eyes the slightest bit.

"Guy, Z, nice to meet you," I say, turning toward the door that leads to the boxing ring.

"Mr. Creed?" Guy says.

I turn my head.

"Your gym bag?" he says.

"Oh, right."

I hand it to him. The bag is an ancient leather boxing duffel, circa 1919, with a single compartment, accessed by a zipper that runs the full length on top of the bag. Guy unzips it, looks inside.

Z says, "What's he got, usual assortment of guns, knives and bombs?" He laughs.

Guy holds the bag open so Z can see the contents.

Z frowns and shakes his head. "Dude. If you're here to fight Billy "the Kid" King, you oughta turn around and haul ass before he sees you."

"Why's that?"

"He's a three-time former Golden Gloves champion. And he's half your age."

I nod.

Z looks exasperated. "And he's never been beat."

"So far," I say.

Z turns to his friend and says, "You believe this guy?"

Guy says, "What'd he do, push you in the street? Embarrass you in front of your girlfriend? Then challenge you to a fight?"

"He made an unsavory remark about my therapist."

Z says, "Your *therapist?*"

I nod.

"What, are you *nuts* or somethin'?"

"Somethin'."

"And you mouthed off to him?"

"Nope. My therapist did. Then she slapped him."

"So what happened?"

"He broke her nose."

Guy says, "Sounds like Billy."

Z says, "You *saw* it? You were *there?*"

I smile and say, "Had I been there, Billy wouldn't be *here*. He'd be in the hospital, or dead."

Z laughs. "You're big, I'll give you that. And you look tough, and *talk* tough."

"And he's got confidence," Guy adds.

"He's got that in spades," Z agrees. "But Billy ain't never been beat. And like I say, he's half your age."

I nod. "Thanks, guys."

Guy says, "Wait. He's got this move." Then he demonstrates a left hook to the body, followed by a left hook to the chin.

"Thanks," I say. "I'll look for it."

DONOVAN CREED

DONOVAN CREED works as an assassin for an elite branch of Homeland Security. When he isn't killing terrorists, he moonlights as a hit man for the mob, and tests torture weapons for the Army. Donovan Creed is a very tough guy.

MEET THE AUTHOR

John Locke is the firs
writer to sell over a millio
self-published ebooks o
Amazon. Every ebook h
has written and publishe
has been a bestseller. Vis
www.donovancreed.com

1
DONOVAN CREED
LETHAL PEOPLE
2 MILLION COPIES AND COUNTING...
JOHN LOCKE

2
DONOVAN CREED
LETHAL EXPERIMENT
2 MILLION COPIES AND COUNTING...
JOHN LOCKE

3
DONOVAN CREED
SAVING RACHEL
2 MILLION COPIES AND COUNTING...
JOHN LOCKE

4
DONOVAN CREED
NOW & THEN
2 MILLION COPIES AND COUNTING...
JOHN LOCKE

5
DONOVAN CREED
WISH LIST
2 MILLION COPIES AND COUNTING...
JOHN LOCKE

6
DONOVAN CREED
A GIRL LIKE YOU
2 MILLION COPIES AND COUNTING...
JOHN LOCKE

7
DONOVAN CREED
VEGAS MOON
2 MILLION COPIES AND COUNTING...
JOHN LOCKE

8
DONOVAN CREED
THE LOVE YOU CRAVE
2 MILLION COPIES AND COUNTING...
JOHN LOCKE

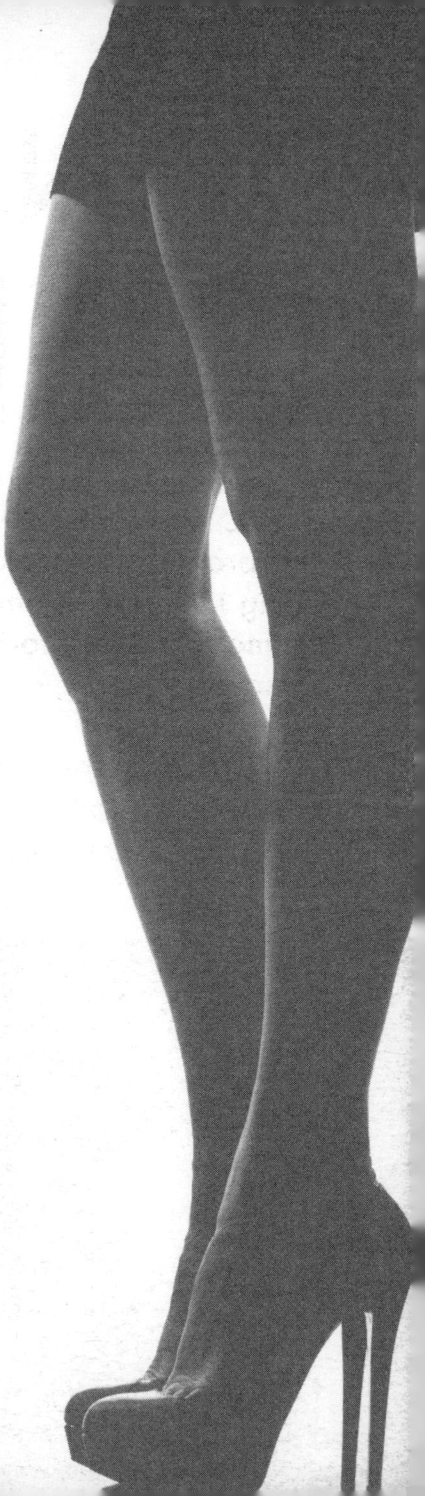